JACOB

ALEXANDER SHIFTER BROTHERS
BOOK THREE

SELINA COFFEY

LOVY BOOKS

Lovy Books Ltd
20-22 Wenlock Road
London N1 7GU

Cover by SC Creative

Jacob

New Orleans, Louisiana

$\mathcal{J}$acob moved deeper into the shadows of the dead-end street, the old buildings around him damp in the fog found so often in New Orleans. His black hair and eyes, paired with his black clothing, helped him to blend into the darkness. Pulling his hand away from something slimy on the wall, the tall man wondered how much more of his life would be spent in the shadows. They were a welcoming place for Jacob, a normal habitat for the middle Alexander brother, but he preferred the warmth and light of sunshine. Always in the shadows, always playing the caretaker, Jacob now found himself once again doing as his older brother, Cade, bid him.

Of late, Jadrian was at the center of Cade's bidding. As if it weren't bad enough that the entire clan and the shifter world were in danger, Jadrian was messing around with vampires, using their blood as a drug. The vampires had always known their blood could cause euphoria and intoxication to non-vampires but had kept it secret, until five years ago.

As the non-magical world sought better and more exotic drugs to make their reality disappear, the vampires started to use their own blood for astronomical profits. The international magical community had criticized the vampires' attempts at ensnaring humans into yet another drug habit and the vampires had finally agreed that only the most discreet and richest of humans would have the luxury of purchasing the drug, their very own blood.

As though addicts are ever truly discreet, Jacob thought to himself, as he softly stalked along the wall, finally spotting his quarry.

He could have shifted into a tiny insect or a black-bird to make his endeavor stealthier, but Jacob preferred to stay in his human form. He didn't like the way his thoughts turned animalistic when he shifted, less human, and less compassionate. At times animalism was needed, it would likely be needed in the future, but for now he preferred to keep his human form.

Trying to resist the urge to pull away from the damp wall, the night air hot but still somehow cold, he listened to the conversation taking place in the box shaped dead-end, using the corner of the building as a blind.

"You're needing more than usual Jadrian, what's getting to you?" The vampire, typical black-haired and pale skinned, asked his brother, his lacy cuffs swinging as the vampire swept back his black hair.

Jacob rolled his eyes at the effeminate gesture. Geez, these vampires and their affectations, could they be bigger stereotypes? Jacob wondered if he dyed it. Could vampires dye their hair? He realized he needed to learn more about the group than what he'd learned through overheard conversations, films, and books over the years. In his early thirties, Jacob didn't have much time for reading anything that wasn't about business matters, but decided he'd have to look in the library of the Sanctuary, an old monastery, when he got back there later.

"It's been a tough time lately. Just give me what I came for and fuck off with the chitchat, Aidan, I don't have time for it tonight." Jadrian was tall and Nordic-looking, with the physique to go along with it. He brushed Aidan's hand away from his own blonde hair. Jadrian was staring daggers at the vampire when Jacob peeked around the corner.

Standing in the shadows, wondering if it was a slug he had just squished beneath his hand, Jacob cringed. Jadrian was usually calm but when somebody pushed his hothead button he could go nuclear. Jacob, always calm, a kinder and gentler version of his brothers, would have dealt with the situation differently, but he wasn't the one buying vampire blood. Jadrian was, and his rush to get back to the cloisters could prove deadly if he didn't calm his shit.

Jadrian's eyes were as cold as his words as he flicked the vampire's hand away, their green depths so icy they were almost clear. Jacob knew pissing off the vampires wasn't a good idea. He saw his brother's eyes go blank and quietly shook his head in satisfaction.

There you go, brother. Calm, collected. Don't piss them off. Jacob's thoughts cut off once again as the vampire gave Jadrian a sultry smile, the light amber of his eyes almost painful looking. Jacob wondered if the light hurt the pale orbs but decided it didn't matter when the vampire spoke again.

"Jadrian, you know you can get this at a much cheaper price, you just need to…" The vampire waved a hand slowly in front of himself, using his eyes to give Jadrian a decidedly sultry look.

Jacob had to assume Jadrian knew the rest of the request because he didn't. The vampire could be asking for anything; sex, information, anything. The dark-haired brother, the adopted brother of the blonde god in the alley, leaned in closer, trying to catch the vampire's meaning.

"I don't think so, Aidan. Just give me the VB and let's get out of here. This damp is starting to annoy me." Jadrian stepped back, his hands going to the back of the tight skinny jeans he wore, sliding down into the pockets in a manner that screamed he didn't give a fuck what the vampire had on offer. He shifted on booted feet and held out his hand, the paleness of his skin not coming anywhere near to matching that of the vampire's.

"Very well, Jadrian. But be careful. Too much of anything is not good for you." The vampire held a long-nailed, slim finger in front of his own face and shook his head disapprovingly. With a nod of his head the vampire indicated to the four gathered goons he'd brought with him that it was time to give Jadrian what he came for.

Jadrian handed over a thick envelope and looked inside the velvet bag the vampire handed him.

"There are only three vials here. I gave you enough for five!" Jadrian's features, relieved only seconds before, rearranged to an angry glare, staring down the Phlebo.

Jacob knew Jadrian would not use the term around the vampire, a shortened form of the term Phlebotomist, used disparagingly for the vampire blood dealers. He could see Jadrian was stringing it along with other nasty words in his mind though. This could get tense.

"The price went up. Demand is growing. Take it or leave it." Aidan shrugged nonchalantly and Jadrian clenched his jaw, the hard line not taking away from the beauty of his features. The massive size of the human, or the strength within his mass, didn't frighten the vampire and Jadrian knew it. Jacob could see Jadrian struggling to control his anger but finally he did.

Jacob sighed, knowing it was done now. He could leave and report back to Cade at the cloister in Bayou Rose, just outside of the city. His mind went to the coming confrontation, and his elder brother's anger, when he turned to walk out of the alley.

A woman stood behind him, watching him curiously with her head cocked. She was pale, as pale as Aidan, and quiet. Her dark hair just as Gothic, but blue eyes lined in black eyeliner and heavy dark shadow. Rather than making her appear awkward and messy, the makeup highlighted how beautiful she was, and her beauty was captivating. Jacob instinctively knew she was a vampire and therefore dangerous. He kept his mouth shut and prepared to shift.

"What is it you hope to see, little spying blackbird?" Her voice was controlled, tight, but somehow high. But pleasingly so, femininely so.

She must be with the dealer, that Aidan guy, Jacob

thought. His heart started to pound so loudly in his chest he wondered if she could hear it. She was so very... captivating. He was so enraptured by her that he couldn't speak, he could only stare. He didn't know if it was her disconcerting gaze, her beauty, or fear of being caught that made his heart race but his instinct told him to shift. His instinct screamed at him to shift, to fly away quickly, but she was so lovely in her black leather pants and light blue bustier that he couldn't think. Her breasts overfilled the top, more than even his own large hands could take in and he stared for a moment before his gaze moved. Her pale shoulders were exposed to the damp night air, as she stood on six inch, knee-length black leather boots. Her long black hair covered her back down to her waist, and long black feathers on delicate silver chains adorned her ears. Jacob decided she was a formidable picture of deadly innocence. She should look like some ridiculous caricature of a Hollywood block-buster but the look suited her. She wore it all well.

Her beguiling gaze, her alluring body and her enchanting voice were dangerous, a danger he couldn't afford to be enthralled by. Vampires were weapons of seduction, meant to entrance their victims. Jacob knew this wasn't a weak woman; she was a vampire that could snap his neck in the blink of an eye and if she was with the Phlebos then he was in grave danger. She glided up to stand close to him, her breasts just barely touching his own chest. If he breathed hard enough to expand his chest he would actually touch the gorgeously pale globes. She was tall as well. He looked into her eyes and shivered. He couldn't look away.

"You are a handsome fellow, blackbird, but I thought you were someone else. All of you Alexanders look so alike. It is intriguing, wondering just how alike you are."

The unnamed vampire brushed a finger down his face, the nail long and tapered. He felt drawn to her, a desire coursing through him unlike anything he had ever felt before.

He tried to make a reply, to tell her to leave him alone, but he could only stare because his tongue was too heavy to move, hoping the reaching finger would touch his lips, quench his need to know what she would taste like.

"You are intriguing enough on your own, blackbird. Shall I take you home with me? Make you mine in your own gilded cage? Or maybe you should fly away before it's too late." She had somehow stepped even closer, her breathy words making him ache deep in his groin, in his heart, in his mind. He wanted to reach for her, he wanted to run away. But he also wanted to find out if she tasted of the peaches her breath smelled of.

Jacob fought with himself, fought to move, to control his flaming desire but felt as though he was losing. Shifters and vamps do not mix, after all. She continued to stare at him, her eyes imploring, drawing him in, and he knew he could drown in those eyes if he allowed himself.

Wake up, move damnit! Jacob screamed the words in his mind but couldn't move and he couldn't speak. He was frozen in place and panicking. She wasn't the best company he could keep and her magnetic stare proved that more than anything; in fact, he was in a whole lot of danger.

Realizing he was being hypnotized by the vampire, her staring gaze her best weapon, Jacob finally shifted. For a fraction of a second he feared he would not be able to shift but he felt the whoosh as his body changed and he flew away.

Up, swiftly up, Jacob flew in the blink of an eye. There was no long, scream-filled bout of adjustment as his bones and muscles twisted into his new shape. Jacob simply made a decision and he was what he wanted; a flying shadow in the darkness. Although his shadow cast a much larger, much darker shape than he had intended.

Rather than shifting into the blackbird she had accused him of being, as he had intended in a sarcastic "fuck you" to the vampire, he had shifted into the shape he was most at home in. The black and red speckled shape of the dragon he knew only he could become.

Beginning to lose his own human thoughts to the dragon-form, Jacob flew in the direction of home and his brother. Cade was safety, Cade was power, Cade would keep the vampire at bay, even in the heart of the American Magical Court. He needed to get back to Cade.

Jadrian

JADRIAN WANTED nothing more than to head back to Kansas, where he could buy all the VB he wanted without greedy vampires stiffing him for the drug he needed to keep up with his shifter brothers. He knew he shouldn't be buying VB but he needed it sometimes, to keep him going, to give him the stamina humans simply didn't possess. He needed the hit of power, strength and euphoria the vampire blood offered. Tonight was a big night.

As a human he didn't have the stamina of his brothers, but he would never tell them that. He would never admit his weakness to them, so he used VB to get him through the hardest times. Jadrian knew he needed it now more than ever; a lot was riding on his shoulders. The pressure was building inside of him as the weight became heavier, the need for the blood growing with each day.

The Mungons, his family's long time enemy,

destroyer of his parents, and hopeful destroyers of the world, had finally come out of hiding and the motorcycle gang they were using as operatives were on the warpath after Cade turned some of their clan over to the magical court. He was on his way there to testify, he just had to get some VB first. Anything to get him through all of this.

As his driver drove the car away from New Orleans, Jadrian caught his reflection in the black tinted window. Tall, handsome and powerful looking, he doubted anyone would guess he had a VB habit. Not one so strong, anyway. He knew he was playing a dangerous game, but he had to. Sometimes his brothers were awake for days, their bodies only needing sleep after a solid week without rest. They could battle for hours but Jadrian couldn't. They'd discovered it during the practices they held every day, that is until he found VB.

Jadrian's body wasn't so strong as Cade's, Kane's or Jacob's. He was trained, physically and emotionally, to withstand a lot of stress and to be able to cope in battle situations, but he just didn't have the stamina. Not without VB anyway.

The driver pulled into the portico hanging over the part of the drive that went by the house and stopped. A doorman opened his door and Jadrian stepped out of the car, straightening the slim black suit he wore, the tight pants tighter than he would like but apparently the current style. Cade had insisted the brothers wear only the best, and that they make an impression, so here he was in the ugliest pair of pants he'd ever seen, something a man should never wear. Presumably the ladies liked the monstrosities though, even if he did feel like his voice kept going a few octaves higher when he shifted and the pants pinched his testicles.

"Such silly, sissy things these pants. Ugh, where's my assistant, I need to change out of these atrocities." Jadrian looked around but rather than seeing his assistant he spotted Cade and his wife, Jacqui. There was a woman with them, a tall redhead with a penchant for flowy green dresses, it seemed. She was beautiful, breath-taking, a Celtic queen with blue eyes if he had ever seen one.

He watched the way she stared at Jacqui and Cade rapturously but Jadrian knew she was barking up the wrong tree there. Cade and Jacqui only had eyes for each other; nobody could intrude on those two. Jadrian shook himself as they approached him, the woman still staring at Jacqui as she spoke quietly to her.

"There you are Jadrian. You will be called momentarily, do you need a moment?" Cade didn't even introduce him to the woman, just shuffled him to the bathroom, whispering quickly.

"Do not volunteer information, speak truthfully, and be sure to keep your answers short here, Jade. These people can make you disappear with a snap of their fingers."

Jadrian nodded and disappeared into the bathroom, his hands going to his suit pocket to pull out the vials. One was good enough for now. Jadrian emptied the vial down his throat and stared into the mirror, waiting for the blood to work its magic. The transformation was instant, so quick he could see it happening as the lines disappeared from around his eyes and mouth and his cheeks took on a healthy color. Even the tiredness that had hollowed out his eyes and cast shadows there was gone.

Feeling restored once more Jadrian straightened his suit and walked out, ready to meet his fate. And the beautiful woman all but sniffing Jacqui's lovely blonde hair. He snorted to himself, she could bark all she wanted to, she wasn't getting up that tree.

Of course, he told himself, she wasn't going to go for him either, no matter how appealing she might find him. If she would ever look away from Cade long enough to see Jadrian she would look right past him. Shifter women didn't marry or mate with non-shifters. It just never happened. Shifter males might marry non-shifters, but the females they chose were usually independent and strong, traits not always valued by human males.

Jadrian watched the woman, her walk more of a strut

than a glide, her hips pleasingly wide and along with her long hair, proclaimed her all woman but her bearing and her gaze said there was far more to this woman than her gender. Was she an Alpha's wife? She had the kind of regal bearing many females with Alpha mates took on.

Jadrian's nostrils flared as he caught her scent, something about the gentle flowery scent not only contradicting but alluring. He felt as though he were being tugged into her and when her eyes crashed into his he felt his heart stop. Shifter or not he knew this woman had to be his; she was most definitely the one. Whether he was ready for settling down or not fate had just changed his entire path and put this woman into his story.

"Ready?" Cade looked at Jadrian nervously and for a moment Jadrian examined his brother's face with a hint of worry.

Had Cade finally figured out how Jadrian was keeping up? Did he use too much? He felt extraordinary, powerful, virile, but perhaps he'd overdone it. He shifted on his feet uncomfortably and nodded.

"I'm as ready as I'll ever be, brother. Show me the way." Jadrian followed Cade, nodding his head at both women as they passed.

Jadrian walked down the long stone passage reminiscent of old English castles, and almost laughed. If they'd only put in torches the effect would be perfect. He even felt a chill in the air that shouldn't be there. He nodded his head at his brother Kane and his wife, Damesha, and carried on down the long hall. Finally they came to a side door and Jadrian was ushered into a room that had recessed lighting.

A large dimly-lit room, the area was filled with rows of tables and had obviously been furnished to bring the eye to the front dais. On the dais were two ancient thrones of carved oak decorated with gold-leaf that had all but worn off. The seat and part of the backs were covered in red velvet and upon them sat the current heads of the magical world. Not royalty but more than simple elected officials. The magical world had had no royals for over a century, this couple stood in their place.

Rumors had swirled for centuries about who the couple was but there was no name in any language for what they were. Many thought they were vampires because the couple was so pale, but they also gave off an aura of shifter. Others said they sensed something else about the couple and could only name it as dread.

Both had long pale hair, almost white, and clear colorless eyes that gave them the appearance of being blind. Jadrian shivered as he looked at the pair. Their voice was the worst part. Voice because even though they were two separate people their voice came out as only one. Jadrian watched their discussion with the man before him, trying to figure out how, despite both mouths moving at the same time, only one voice came out. It was just too freaky and he had to look away.

"Jadrian Alexander! You are called before the court!" That creepy voice, not masculine but not feminine boomed loudly through the long room.

He moved up to a long blue carpet edged in gold, his head bowed as he approached the dais. Once he got to a spot marked on the carpet with two gold circles he knelt. Cade had taught him the procedure earlier in the day. Protocol was everything here and this wasn't the place to display the cocky attitude he usually gave the world.

"And what do you come to tell us, Jadrian Alexander?"

The voice gave him the willies and Jadrian tried to repress a shiver. Yeah, these two weren't getting his patented cocky smile that could make a woman's panties fall off or a man doubt his sexuality for a moment.

"I have come to give witness about the Mungons and their activities over the last few weeks." His head was still bowed, following the protocol that stated that he couldn't look up until they allowed it. Fuck, this sucked, bowing and scraping before people who weren't even royalty. Not cool.

"We know what they are doing. We have interviewed enough people about them now. You are not a magical, why are you here?" The voice sounded bored but curious and Jadrian shifted, his knees beginning to protest, even with the VB.

"You called me here." Jadrian had to fight the urge to add "duh" to the end of his sentence. He usually wasn't one for protocol or holding his tongue but, as Cade had said, these people could zap him out of existence.

"Indeed." There was a bit of a harrumph, as though the voice knew he'd mentally added that "duh", after all. There was a moment of quiet as the ancient pair shifted on their thrones. "What do you think of all of this, as a non-magical, Jadrian Alexander?"

"Pardon?" He couldn't believe they were asking his opinion.

"You seem a brave but intelligent fellow. You are here, after all, before us. We are curious as to your thoughts, as a non-magical. How will their activities impact the non-magical world, and us?"

Jadrian was shocked enough to spread his hands out before him, not sure how to answer. They were waiting, though, so he tried to form an answer.

"I believe they want a war, majesties. The Mungons want to eliminate most of the shifters and whoever is left will be used as slaves, as will the vampires. For some reason they believe they can overthrow you, wipe out most of the non-magical population on the planet, and set themselves up as overlords. They want to enslave the world and set themselves up as the ultimate kings, with only the few needed to give them what they need to survive and control the remaining population."

"Indeed."

Jadrian was starting to see that the word was used as filler, to buy them a moment to allow them to think.

"They have to be stopped or we all face a stark and rather bleak future, if we survive to see it." He spoke bluntly but carefully. "Whether they do the unthinkable and find a way to oust you or they only succeed in part, they will cause chaos between the magical and non-magical worlds with their machinations. They must be stopped before it gets that far."

"Thank you, Jadrian Alexander. That is all. You words are blunt but honest and we appreciate your candor. You may take your leave." The king waved a hand from his seat on the left as the queen nodded her head as though she had made a decision. "We shall take a break and return within an hour. You may all go."

The room began to empty and Jadrian gave a sigh of relief as he stood. The windowless room had started to feel like a coffin the longer he'd knelt there but now he could breathe again. He'd kept his wits about him, answered honestly, and now he was done. Done and still alive, all a man could ask for really.

With a jaunty wave he found Cade in the crowd and

joined him. Cade slapped his brother's shoulder and shook his hand.

"You did great. Maybe more ballsy than you have a right to be but it worked. Good call." Cade guided his brother into the crowd leaving the hall.

"What do you mean?" Jadrian had never been summoned for the king and queen before, he didn't know he had done anything extraordinary.

"You told them the truth. Most would have chosen to keep most of that to themselves."

"What?" Jadrian looked at his brother with shock, had he been nearer to death than he thought?

"People have been zapped for less. Sometimes they respond favorably to blunt honesty, but most of the time, it is the old zap. You must have impressed them."

Jadrian felt his knees go weak but he steadied himself. Damn, that was close.

2

Jacob

Jacob wandered the halls, at a loose end now Cade was in a meeting. Normally, Jacob made it a point to report to Cade immediately upon his return from a mission but his brother was overseeing Jadrian as he met with the royal rulers of the magical world. Jacob shivered and ran a hand through his black hair, remembering his own meeting with the overly tall couple.

Jacob was over six feet tall but the couple both stand over seven feet tall. And their appearance was, well, gross! He shivered again, glad that he wasn't here in the bayous with them every day. Give him Kansas any day of the week.

Moonlight shot into the windows lining the long

passageway as he passed each one, sparkling at him in long winks as he went by. The night was growing old now and soon the sun would burst across the horizon, brightening the day. Another night of little sleep and a lot of work. Wanting nothing more than a hot bath to sink into, Jacob headed for his room, little more than a cell situated somewhere down this hallway, he was sure.

The long halls of the former monastery, built in the 18th century in a rather Gothic style, were unsettling and echoed even the slightest of sounds. The dark building was entirely intimidating and exuded an air of menace. Jacob assumed it was something the magicals thought of to scare off curious humans. Why else would you want such a frightening atmosphere in a place where the magical world came together for peace?

With a confused look he realized he had missed his room somewhere, he was too far down the hall. He was turning back when he realized he wasn't alone. Standing about ten feet away was her—that woman—the vampire woman. His brow creased even further as he saw her. He wasn't afraid of her, he knew he could get away, but why was she here?

"Shouldn't you be crawling into a hole to avoid the sunlight by now?" He hadn't meant the words to come out so acerbically but they did. He watched her as he waited for her response, ignoring the tall brunette male standing behind her in the shadows. Jacob didn't recognize the other vampire and assumed he was a flunky of the woman before him.

Somehow she looked softer here, not so dangerous and deadly, and not so capable of fiendish things that made his skin crawl. No, now she was far more alluring, beautiful certainly, but different somehow, some of her sexuality gone with the lack of danger. That didn't mean she wasn't intoxicating, far from it. He still felt a pull to her, a need for her that defied logic.

"I thought you flew away, little blackbird." Her words were just as soft but her voice didn't hold that lacy veil of venom as it had earlier. She stared at him, as though he were a bug she was about to eat.

Why had she dropped the attempt to hypnotize him, he wondered as he realized that was the difference between now and their earlier meeting. Had she figured out it didn't work as well on shifters as it did on humans? Jacob didn't feel afraid, he was a shifter after all. He could get out of most situations, but he was intrigued by her and that could be just as dangerous as her attempts to mesmerize him. Jacob examined her as time stretched out between them, the silence growing long.

"Why are you here?" He wondered aloud, his hands itching to explore the bare expanse of her shoulders. Dressed in a black dress that pushed the top of her breasts up high while flaring out around her thighs, she was seductive, her pale skin almost too white to be real. Jacob couldn't look away and wondered if he was incredibly wrong about her ability to mesmerize him. She walked towards him, stalking her prey. Was she going to kiss him? Somehow it didn't surprise him that he still felt the longing to taste her lips.

He only had eyes for those plump ruby lips as she stilled in front of him, her breasts pushing into his chest. She didn't touch him as she looked up; she just stood there, her eyes drilling into his. Jacob felt a deep ache, low in his abdomen as she stared up at him, her face impassive, far too seductive. He wanted her.

"Kiss me." She whispered the plea and Jacob couldn't say no. He forgot that he'd been looking for his room. He forgot he still needed to report to Cade. He let his world become the woman as his lips found hers. He didn't know why, he hadn't been hypnotized but wondered if maybe he had because he'd never felt lips so soft, never kissed a woman that tasted so deliciously of peaches. That was almost his undoing, the taste of her, and he felt a strong urge to push her against the wall and drive himself deep into her depths. He held the urge off, fighting with himself until the soft push of her breasts against his chest sent him into the abyss.

He moved with the power of a shifter and instantly they were against the wall, his hand sliding under the thigh that wrapped around his back as he pushed into her, cradling himself in her heat. She made a soft sound of delight and it made his pulse jump. He needed to be inside her, he thought, as his lips sought hers.

All that existed was this woman, this vampire, and his need to taste every inch of her. He wasn't even upset when a man came up beside them in the very public hallway, cupping her breast in his large palms even as Jacob continued to kiss her. He knew the man was there, adding to her pleasure, heightening his with it, creating possibilities of things to come.

Jacob pulled away and looked at the man. All he could focus on was the man's brownish gold eyes and the challenge in them. That challenge asked if Jacob was man enough, if he could take her on with another man present. The man was handsome, but also a vampire. Would he survive the encounter?

Vampires and shifters didn't usually mingle but there were no restrictions on the act of sex. A shifter took their life into their own hands, much as humans did, when they mated with vampires, however. Shifter blood didn't have the intoxicating qualities that vampire blood had on shifters, but they could drink it much the same as human blood. Was this the plan, then? Get him alone and suck him dry? A shiver passed through him at the thought of the woman sucking another part of him dry.

Jacob blinked, looked past her eyes down to her lips. Pulling her to him once more, Jacob thrust his tongue deep into her mouth, pressing her to him and trapping the man's hands between them. Challenge accepted.

Jacob was normally a mild-tempered man, always in his brothers' shadows, but he'd never been one to turn down a challenge. This woman was pure challenge. His body was strong, shifter strong and physically strong; he could defend himself if need be. The air of danger heightened his need rather than dampened it. He could take them both on, if it meant he got to fuck her until she screamed his name.

What he'd seen in the man's eyes was something he thought he'd never be offered, a chance of a lifetime, and that challenge had been reflected in her eyes. Jacob, his brain now doing little more than answering his body's demands, followed them as they led him to a chamber far away from his own.

He followed quietly, his mind already providing images of what was to come, what he hoped was about to come. He watched the sway of her bottom and felt his groin tighten, soon that part of her would be bare, he'd feel her silky skin and perhaps see the black garters she wore stretching across it.

He loved a woman in a garter belt and stockings.

They arrived at a larger chamber, much finer than his bare monk's cell, with a fireplace along an inner wall. The room, lit only by the fire, was draped in velvets and furs, expensive coverings designed to keep the occupant warm. Perhaps vampires felt the cold more than he realized. Louisiana was a hot place to live but something about the monastery kept it at a little above freezing all year round, even in the depths of summer. Could the bone-chilling cold reach a vampire's core?

Jacob squinted at the woman for a moment as she went to a drinks tray and prepared three drinks. What was her name? She looked as though she would have an exotic name, perhaps something Slavic or Italian. Maybe something even far more ancient, Mesopotamian or even Phoenician. She didn't appear ancient but something about her gave off the impression that she knew things that man had long ago forgotten.

Jacob shook himself, the moment passing as her fingers brushed his to get him to take his glass.

"Stop daydreaming, blackbird." Her voice was as intoxicating as the rest of her. Her fingers wandered down his chest, lower to his abdomen, and lower still, beneath the button of his pants.

Jacob held his breath as her fingers played there, teasing him with small circles that kept going lower.

"We have all night, all of eternity, but I want you focused. I want you to know what I am doing to you." Her words were a spell, drawing his gaze to her lips and he bent forward, wanting to taste the sweet peaches of her lips once more.

She allowed the caress, a soft brush of flesh against

flesh, and pushed her hand deeper into his pants. When she flattened her palm over his very hard length, he shuddered. The coolness of her skin was a sharp contrast to the heat of his own. She wasn't as cold as he thought she might be, she was rather warm, really, but there was a coolness in her hand that appeased the heat in his groin, soothed it. His breath shook in his chest as his eyes burned into hers. This was really going to happen.

"I want to know. But if you don't want me to bend you over that table and fuck you until you can't scream my name anymore, I suggest you take your hands out of my pants." His words came out roughly, the passion she'd stirred adding a tightness to his throat, but she gave him a pleased smile.

She still pulled her hand out of his pants, a move that made Jacob groan in protest but made the other man in the room groan in pleasure.

"Orgasm denial can be very sweet you know." The man's words were sibilant, his voice almost feminine.

Was he gay? Jacob wondered as he looked the man over. Tall, with sex oozing from his every pore the man was definitely gothic in dress but his eyes promised an ancient pleasure, a modern take on an old act. Jacob was willing to find out what the man had to offer and didn't question his decision. Sex was sex, wherever you found it. Normally he took it from pliant women who didn't want attachments, just sex and a goodbye.

Jacob could see that the man's chest was as broad as his own but the man was slightly taller. His hair, not dyed the normal gothic black, was still in a long straight sheet down his back, the light brown shining with golden hues that matched his eyes. He also wasn't a thin string of a man, rather he appeared to be strong, well-shaped, and healthy, even if his skin was the requisite pale shade of alabaster.

Jacob wanted to dismiss the man but he was intrigued. He'd never been with a man but this male creature was tempting. What did he offer, exactly, this pale god of sexuality?

"Whatever you like, my queen's blackbird. I will give you whatever you want." The voice held dark promise and sweet anticipation.

Jacob's eyes narrowed on the man, the deep voice pleasing his ears in a way a male's voice had never pleased him before. Right in his cock. But how had he known Jacob's thoughts? Intuition? Observation of the speculation on Jacob's face?

The woman returned and Jacob, normally careful and cautious, took a swig of her offered drink. He held the empty glass back to the woman. He didn't want to be drunk but he wanted to numb some of his inhibitions.

He wanted to let himself enjoy it. Alcohol would dull any lingering worries.

"One more, but I want your clothes off before you finish it." Her words made his cock throb in his pants.

"Will you need help or are you the only one that gets to touch this wonderful specimen, my queen?" The vampire looked at Jacob appreciatively as Jacob began to remove his clothes.

Jacob paused, watching the woman as she poured, her face turned away. What would her answer be? Jacob realized he really did find the idea of the man joining them, touching him, quite intriguing but apparently the decision was up to her. No matter how hard his cock might be at the thought of the man's lips on his bare flesh.

With a wave of her hand the female dismissed the male's words, not bothering to turn around yet.

"Tonight, he is mine. Perhaps another time, my darling. But you are certainly welcome to watch." She finally turned, coming back with a glass of bourbon to a very naked Jacob. "Mmm, nice, blackbird."

She ran her fingers down his chest, making him choke on the drink as his throat responded to her touch. He gained control of himself and finished swallowing, his eyes on a slim finger with a pointed black-lacquered nail. He still didn't know her name.

Jacob's nerves strung tight, and on the edge of snapping as her nail scraped down his bare nipple, wound even tighter. He wasn't ashamed of his nudity, he stood proudly before her penetrating gaze and approving nod. He just had to control his own hands for the moment or they would be fighting, vampire against shifter, for control. He was willing to let her have her way with him. For now.

He could sense she needed this from him, she needed to feel superior, so he would allow it but only for the moment. He may only be a minor player in the Alexander family but that was only a mistake of birth. Jacob knew he was a power unto himself and had learned to keep his own secrets, to rein in his own thoughts and skills, to let the others have their glory. He didn't mind his place in the shadows but with her, soon enough he would show her exactly who he was. If he ever learned her name, that is.

Something about the game, the anonymity of it, made his blood sing in his veins, and he liked the sensation. There was no rush to find out her name for now. He loved the mystery of it all, and when her lips kissed the flesh above his left nipple, he thought he would burst on the spot. Just her lips grazing his heated skin had nearly set him off, something that had never occurred in his entire life, even as an awkward teenager. Jacob always maintained control.

She'd teased him for far too long and now he just

wanted to be buried in her hot cleft, his hips thrusting into her ass as he took her from behind. The thought of those garters, peeking out from under the short hem of her dress, spurred his fantasy on. Her fingers, stilled as she had kissed him, ran up the smooth curve of his shoulders, down his back, and over the solid plane of his sculpted ass. Jacob couldn't stop the way his hips pushed into her softness, telling her without words what he needed.

"You may touch me now."

Jacob didn't realize he had been waiting for permission until she gave it.

His hands went around her waist as her lips encircled his nipple, her sharp teeth, all razor sharp, biting with a gentleness he hadn't thought she'd be capable of. He gasped once more, a swear word this time, and thrust into her again.

"Eager are we?" She gave a chortle of laughter as her tongue flicked at the tight bud, her hands squeezing his ass appreciatively. He heard a low sound of satisfaction come from her and thrust into her once more, his cock rocking into her soft abdomen.

"Very. You have teased me long enough, or do you think I am made of stone?" He felt his pulse in his ears, felt his heart racing in his chest, and had to fight with himself not to tear off her dress.

"Oh, you will be inside me soon, blackbird. Relax."

She snapped her fingers as she stared into his eyes and the male came, pulling her clothes away gently, leaving only her garter belt and stockings with the panties beneath. The male cupped her breasts from behind as Jacob stared. She was beautiful; a marble statue with high round breasts, a slim waist, and flared hips. Her legs were sensual creations of muscle, curves and long lines he couldn't wait to have wrapped around his head. She was also bare, not a single stray hair anywhere on her body.

"Gorgeous." He breathed the word as she shuddered in the male's arms, her nipples pinched between his long pale fingers. They looked at Jacob, both imploring him to take the nipple the male offered, to take her.

Jacob took her by her waist, pulling her from the man. His powerful arms lifted her, pulling her up until his lips wrapped around the dark red of her tight nipple, and he felt her shudder once more.

He knew her need was growing, he could smell it in the air as her flesh heated from a deathly chill to a level somewhere around the normal human body temperature. Her skin smelled like the peaches her mouth tasted of, and her pulse raced, some unnamed person's blood running in her veins. The thought didn't dissuade Jacob, rather it spurred him on, to seek out the danger she offered him.

The male backed away as Jacob moved with her,

carrying her to a chaise lounge, her legs wrapped around his waist. Kneeling between her legs, Jacob prodded her thighs apart, the smooth black velvet of the chaise a softly erotic sensation against his fingers. His eyes explored her secrets, the pinkness of her folds, the tell-tale signs of her arousal as her clit began to swell.

His fingers against her nether lips made her shiver, her breathing coming in halting gasps as he split her open to explore her silky depths, a long finger probing into her. He watched her, stirring her with another finger, until she closed her eyes, her arousal growing. When she sighed blissfully he lowered his mouth and sucked at her with his lips, his tongue laving over her clit, rasping it harshly. He knew she would love it.

And she did, her legs clamped around his legs and her stomach clenched tightly as he repeated the stroke. Her back arched as his fingers plunged into her once again, the seeking rhythm soon settling into a steady pace that made her hips follow, that had her ass coming off the chair.

Jacob watched her greedily, her pleasure his own, and waited for that moment, that sudden lurch, and hummed in satisfaction when her head fell back and her hips lunged into his face. A slow fluttering began in her wet depths and he increased the pressure of his tongue, pressed another finger into her until there were two delving further into her, wanting nothing more than to have her coming all over his face.

In that moment Jacob realized how totally vulnerable he was, engrossed in her arousal, his tattooed back, a back his family never ever saw because of the tattooed dragon sleeping there, bared to the man behind him, and his senses attuned only to her. The male could have taken him then, in any way he liked with a knife or with his dick, and Jacob would not have been aware until the last moment. He shuddered but didn't hesitate to show his fearlessness as he shifted, his powerful hands grasping at her hips to pull her closer as he lunged into her dripping pussy with a cock pulsing for her alone.

She gasped again, the flagging flutters of her walls turning to a tight clamping sensation as he lunged into her roughly, and he loved it. Her eyes blazed open, drilling into his with intensity as he started a brutal pace, a pace a human would not be capable of keeping up with. But she took it and grinned, meeting each of his thrusts with a sharp jolt of her own.

Jacob grinned down at her and briefly wondered if he had met his match. He thrust into her once more, her slick depths even wetter now, and saw her eyes fluttering. She was close again. His thumb traveled down the flat plane of her hip, down to her mound, to find the center of need. Pressing into the bud, he saw her eyes fly open again and knew he'd given her what she wanted.

"Harder," she demanded. "I'm so wet I can't stand it but I need more. Give me more."

"You will get every fucking thing you ask for, sweetness. All you have to do is ask for it." Jacob pressed the organ harder, his thumb bearing down in tight circles as she sat up, pushing her breasts to his face.

"Do not stop fucking me." Demands again but he didn't mind. He took her nipple into his mouth and sucked as hard as he could, until his teeth grazed the sensitive flesh roughly and she cried out in release.

He felt her orgasm breaking, felt her walls pulsing with satisfaction, and groaned.

But Jacob wasn't done yet, he needed to hear her cry out his name, even if it was only the blackbird nickname she'd given him.

He pulled her hips tighter to his, fucking into her at a driving pace, his hips churning against her, his length stroking every possible inch of her. He couldn't get any further inside and he banged into her with a pace she kept up with easily.

Her back was arched as she pressed up onto her elbows, her breasts thrust high into the air and he considered telling the male to get behind her, to cup them, but stopped himself. She had only wanted him. Jacob glanced over, saw the man watching them, his cock hard in his pants but not touching himself. Now that was control!

Jacob wiped sweat from his brow as she climbed higher than before, her pulsing clamping hard around his length and he plunged into her over and over, so hard her breasts were bouncing enticingly on her chest. He loved watching the soft flesh moving, the way her stomach creased as she leaned into him, pressing her tight walls down around him harder.

Jacob wanted to bite her, just enough to make her moan, but he couldn't reach her. He drove his hands beneath her, cupping her ass, his nails biting into her soft flesh there.

"You are fucking beautiful. So hungry, so very hot little vampire queen."

Her eyes popped open, and for a moment he knew he wasn't safe. Her eyes blazed with something he couldn't define but it made him long to give up his own will. He couldn't stop now, though, he couldn't pull out of her, not when he was so very fucking close. He just wanted to get off then he would leave. That was it.

She was there again, her cries growing louder, her walls starting to pulse around him once more, and she sat up, her lips claiming his. Jacob let her take his mouth, her tongue invading his mouth, laying waste to his will to resist her as she groaned a word into his mouth.

"Blackbird, come with me," she urged, her nails brushing at his nipples, scraping them, creating a pain that burned into pleasure as she did it again. He rocked back on his heels, his body rocked by the sensations she gave him. When she pinched the bud between her nails she caused a chain reaction that ended with his dick pulsing inside of her, emptying into her, as his brain exploded into dark shades of nothing.

Jacob considered taking it further, he considered ensuring she was as wrung out as she looked but he was uncharacteristically exhausted. When he fell over, completely unconscious, he wasn't aware of it. The female vampire sat up, looked down at him sadly for a moment, and wiped at her face to smooth the look away, along with the sweat dripping into her eyes. A coldness replaced the tender sadness on her face the male vampire never saw, not that he would admit it anyway.

"Pick him up, let's get him out of here." She told him, steeling her shoulders as she went for a robe to cover her nudity with. The night wasn't done yet.

* * *

JACOB'S HEAD pounded and he groaned in misery as he came awake, dawn barely piercing the small window high above his head. Where the fuck was he and what the fuck had happened? He tried to turn over but his arms were sheathed in metal, as were his legs. Fear overshadowed by anger rocketed through him as he tried to see in the darkness that still ruled the room he was in.

"I tried to warn you, blackbird, but you flew away too quickly. Now it is too late."

He heard her seductive voice in the darkness and memories flooded back into his brain. Her moans of delight as she writhed into his face, the way her nails dug into his ass as she came, flexing into her with a groan as he exploded inside of her. Then darkness. Nothing.

What had she done to him? What was she going to do to him? Jacob stilled on the bed as the sound of metal scraping metal pierced the silence and he strained to pick out lines in the darkness but couldn't see any. Then her voice was in his ear, whispering quietly so that only he could hear.

"I didn't want to do this but we have no choice. You are our only hope. Please do not fight me. You will not win." Something pierced the tender flesh of his right arm and her lips, the lips he had longed to have on his flesh not long ago, began to suck at his arm.

What the fuck was she doing? He wanted to struggle but knew it truly was no use. The clamps around his wrists were made of silver, silver that had been enchanted, even he couldn't break them. Which meant he couldn't shift to get away either.

Suddenly she stopped sucking, a sigh escaping her bloodied lips. He could almost make her out now, the sky brightening just enough to let him see that she was nude and that her lips were stained with his blood.

"You are the dragon shifter. You will be our salvation." Then she began to suck at his arm once more and Jacob gave a silent scream of horror and fear in his head. He knew, wherever he was, that nobody could hear him. Not even Cade with his shifter awareness of all of his brothers could sense him, or save him now. This woman, this vampire, was psychotic, and he was well and truly fucked!

3

Jadrian

"So what's her name?" Jadrian asked the bartender in the lounge room of the Sanctuary, staring at the woman behind him in the mirror across from him on the wall.

"Who?" The bartender, a middle-aged man wearing a black vest, black pants, and a white shirt with rolled up sleeves, plunked a glass of beer in front of Jadrian and looked around. "The redhead?"

"Yeah, the redhead." The redhead was currently giggling with Jacqui, Cade's wife, her hand resting intimately on Jacqui's arm. Jacqui had thawed out then.

"That's Allana, head of the Tuscola Clan." The bartender's eyes held a look of admiration.

"Alpha is she?" Jadrian asked, studying the woman

more deeply. An alpha! Slugging back his beer he left some money for the bartender and stood. "Well, that girl is barking up the wrong tree. Again."

"Might be, but what a tree to bark up."

Jadrian had to agree as he walked away, heading out of the lounge and into the darkened hallways. He hated these things, anybody could sneak up on you.

"Where's Jacob?" The voice came from behind and Jadrian turned to find his oldest brother standing there with the baby of the family, Kane. Kane looked like he was ready to head back to his farm and Jadrian felt ready to go with him. Jadrian and Cade were alike in many ways but not in the looks department. They were very much alike in personality but day and night in the looks department.

Jadrian looked over at his brother, leader of their clan, and gave an exasperated sigh of frustration. He wanted to get back to his room and brood in peace.

"Am I his keeper now? I have no idea where Jacob is. I'll go look for him." Jadrian was feeling frustrated and a bit peevish. Allana, the seductive temptress filling his head with fantasies, seemed to only have eyes for Cade's wife. He'd hunted her down in the dining hall, hoping Jacqui would introduce them. They'd never looked up from whatever deep conversation they were involved in. He'd followed them into the lounge but was still no better off.

Normally Jadrian could intuit Cade's thoughts, years of practice aiding him, but between Allana's lack of interest and the vampire blood, he felt on edge. Cade looked at Jadrian and Jadrian knew he was seeing the anxiety but his brother chose not to comment on it. Jadrian breathed a sigh of relief and went off in search of Jacob, but the beautiful woman took up most of his thoughts.

He wandered the cold halls that even the humid Louisiana heat couldn't penetrate, and cursed under his breath. He wasn't used to feeling like this, it was something totally new. With a deep breath he wondered if this was love at first sight. He laughed to himself, dismissing the idea. He didn't have time for love, for a family, as his brother's adviser and aide. Besides, she didn't even know he was alive. She was barking up the wrong tree, this alluring creature, if she thought Cade and Jacqui would give her the time of day in their bed.

Jacqui and Cade's wedding had come as a shock but Jadrian had kept his thoughts to himself. He'd seen their love for each other bloom and knew, no matter how their relationship started, they were a unit now, deeply in love and committed to each other. Everyone could see that. Well, everyone but the most beautiful woman he'd ever seen, that is.

He'd still not found Jacob so Jadrian walked into the darkness outside of the former monastery. Disconcerting sounds came from the swamp nearby, chirps, growls, and drawn out sounds that were likely the death-cries of small animals, sending a shiver down Jadrian's spine. He doubted Jacob was out in this. Jadrian took a deep breath, trying to clear the redhead from his mind but she stayed resiliently put.

Stalking back into the safety of the building, Jadrian wondered if he'd ever get the woman's attention. He walked back to the sleeping quarters, hoping to report to Cade, and saw his brother, Jacqui and Allana heading into a sleeping chamber. Jadrian went back to the corner he'd just passed and stole a glance around the side. Allana's hand was gently resting on Jacqui's elbow and there was a gleam in her eye, a promise.

Jadrian's head fell back against the stone wall. Had he been wrong? He would have sworn Cade wouldn't allow another woman into his marital bed, but maybe? There was a curiosity about Jacqui, a need to explore that made her a bit wild, but Cade usually provided her with all she needed. Jadrian knew Cade could be possessive, keeping some things for himself. Would he share his wife with anyone else, even a woman, in such an intimate way?

The woman whispered something into Jacqui's ear and his sister-in-law giggled. Jadrian glared, pulling his head back around the corner again, hating the charming woman for a moment. He adored all of his sisters-in-law and though Jacqui had been hard to warm to at first, he would protect her life with his own if it came down to it. He felt treasonous for the moment of disloyalty and headed for the area of the place where he knew he could find some alcohol. It was late but he needed a drink. He obviously would not be speaking to Cade anymore tonight.

He spent an hour staring glumly into the same glass of bourbon, his stomach in knots. Why did she have this effect on him? He hadn't even really spoken to her yet. Was she a witch as well as a shifter?

He decided to give up on the questions for the night when he saw the sun was starting to rise and thought it best to try for some sleep. Heading into the sleeping quarter, he saw Allana coming out of his brother's room. She didn't look as though she had been participating in any kind of adult activity but just the fact that she was walking out of his brother's room in the middle of the night made his stomach tense. He wanted to hit something but balled his fists instead and stalked up to her. Grabbing her wrist he turned her around and only just missed being punched squarely in the head. That vampire blood might make him squiffy sometimes but it sure improved his reflexes.

"What are you up to?" he demanded, his hand clamped around her wrist. She broke the contact easily.

She was a shifter, after all. His fists might be iron but only to a human.

"What the fuck is it to you?" She shot daggers at him with her eyes; angry blue eyes that made his groin tighten with awareness. Fuck, she was hot when she was angry!

"That's my brother's room you have just moseyed out of, missy. Now, what are you up to?" His eyes stared their own daggers. She needed to know just because he was human it didn't mean he could be played. He wasn't going to back down from her haughty attitude, he didn't care if she was the queen of Sheba. This was family and you didn't fuck with family.

"If you must know, "brother dear", we were talking about an alliance between our clans." Her glare had changed to curiosity and a new fire lit the dark blue of her eyes. It seemed she liked a challenge.

"I see. Care to discuss it with me, catch me up over a drink?" He changed tack so quickly she blinked at him for a moment. He'd seen the calculation in her eyes and knew she had some kind of ploy going. His question tripped her up.

She licked her bottom lip and looked him up and down, a move that drew his eyes to her sultry wet lips. He knew she saw a very tall, very blond man with a body most human men would pay their soul to own. Every inch of him was muscled, his skin tanned from a summer of work, with the face to match his body. He knew his looks were exceptional but took it for granted. Most of the time he didn't care, but now he was glad he'd been blessed in that respect.

Staring down at her, his eyes hard, he felt something tighten in his abdomen, something beyond need. Hunger perhaps, a hunger for her? Jadrian kept his face impassive as he looked at her, hoping but not daring to let this woman who bore herself like a queen know his thoughts.

"I have a better idea." He'd seen the moment she made the decision to accept his offer and waited for her counter offer.

Jadrian's heart pounded in his chest, her seductive words making his pulse race as scenarios played through his mind. Scenarios that included a lot of drinking and no clothes.

"What's that?" He threw the question out with no inflection, his tone implying he didn't give a fuck what she had to offer but was humoring her. And pretended he wasn't staring at her lips, imagining them otherwise occupied.

"I have an entire bottle of Scotch in my room. Care to join me?" She'd walked up close to him, her eyebrows rising in question.

She was gorgeous; her heart-shaped face a perfection of peaches and cream. Pale and clear, her skin enhanced her features and the smattering of freckles over the top of her nose were enchanting. Jadrian had to fight to keep from pulling her to his own body and when a painted green fingernail found its way to his chest he couldn't stop the sharp inhalation that gave him away. His nostrils flared as he became hyper-aware of Allana, of how tempting she was, of how much she'd been on his mind since he'd first seen her.

"A bottle you say? And what else do you have planned for the evening, or should I say morning, besides a drink?" His words were a whisper that made her visibly shiver, the timbre of his voice just the right pitch to make his words a sensual promise.

Her response made his own skin feel too tight and he flexed his hands, trying to ease his tension. Playing with shifters could be dangerous, both physically and emotionally. One had to walk on eggshells or risk being little more than a toy to play with, even with the females. He'd learned that long ago.

"Whatever you have in mind." Her full peach lips parted at the end, inviting him in.

What the hell was he supposed to do now, he wondered, as he tried to shove his hands in his trouser pockets. Stupid, sissy skinny jeans were too tight so he stood there with his fingertips in the tight pockets.

Shifters mated with who they chose, when they chose, sometimes even the married ones mated with others. But she had something up her sleeve and he wasn't sure if that was going to benefit his own clan or if it would put them in even more danger than they were already in. She could be working with the Mungons to eradicate his tribe, or perhaps she was trying to use him to get to his brother and the other man's wife? Maybe she was being truthful and she had been discussing an alliance with his brother. Something about her set him on edge and it caused him to doubt what she said. With a tight groin screaming at him to follow her, Jadrian wasn't sure if he should listen to his body or his mind. He wanted her but maybe he'd made a mistake when he'd stopped her in the hallway.

Jacob

JACOB WOKE up in the cell, sunlight barely beaming into the room through the tiny window above him, high on the stone wall. The silver chains were still in place and he groaned, the silver starting to burn after hours of contact with his skin. The chains were thick, brutally thick, and even he wouldn't be able to break through them, not with the enchantment on them. Flinging his head back against the pillow, Jacob wanted to scream, but out loud this time.

"You won't be in the chains for much longer, little blackbird. Soon you'll be one of us and you'll be bound to me and only me. I have begun the process already." Her silky voice came from somewhere around his feet and Jacob shifted, his head swiveling as he looked down his own nude body to the bare woman at the end of the bed.

"What have you done?" Her words had showered him with fear; she could only mean one thing but you had to give permission for what she was suggesting, the magical world required it!

Jacob's fear was forgotten for a moment as his gaze finally found her huddled in a chair at the end of the bed. She looked so vulnerable, so chaste even in her nudity, that his heart melted for a moment. Then cold fury washed over him as she looked up and her gaze caught his.

"I have done what needed to be done, what your brother was too weak to do. The Mungons only grow stronger as we sit here, investigating, making plans, trying to follow our own laws. It's admirable, I'll give Cade that, but this isn't the time for diplomacy. This is the time to attack, to annihilate that which threatens us the most." Her words had grown more vehement as she spoke, the anger, fear, and urgency making him pay attention to her.

"And where do I fit into all of this? Will my blood

make you fertile again and create a child that'll be the chosen one or something?" Jacob scoffed at her and let his head fall back against the pillow again, his body and mind tired out even from the brief exchange. Something was wrong with him.

Jacob became more aware of this as the strength began to ebb away even quicker, he could barely even find the strength to breathe now.

"You'll find out soon enough, Jacob. I'm sorry, but as the queen of my people I had to take matters into my own hands. There is knowledge we have kept from the world, from even the magical world, about a shifter that is unique, that can save us all. Even amongst our kind, the shifter is considered a myth, but the first time I saw you I knew there was something different. I suspected but I wasn't sure until you flew away. You're a dragon shifter!"

Her eyes revealed a bright spark of hope, and Jacob felt as though he'd been plunged into an even deeper well of fear and powerlessness. As his strength ebbed he looked over at his arm. An IV was sending a red liquid into his veins, the line open and running quickly through the process. His eyes widened as he realized his fears were valid, she wasn't only breaking the law, she was destroying him!

"But it's only a myth. Sure, I'm a dragon shifter, but what you're doing is... you can't do this! You don't have my permission!" He pulled at his arm but it was strapped to a board connected to the bed. His other arm would not reach and he was well and truly stuck. He looked back at her pleading. "Please, don't do this to me! I beg you, please!"

The woman, he still didn't know her name, looked away, hiding the heartbreak in her eyes but he saw it. She didn't want to do this but then why was she doing it?

"It has to be done. You will save us all, Jacob. You will become the vampire shifter, the only one capable of surviving the transformation, and you will become the most powerful being on this earth. My king, my minion, and my savior. The savior of us all." She walked away then, leaving him alone as his organs began to fail.

"No! You can't! You'll kill me! It's only a myth!" His words rang out in the cell but not a soul answered him. As he lost the ability to breathe, as he felt his heart begin to stop, Jacob mourned for his brothers, for their families, and for himself. He also mourned for the selfish stupid woman that had done this to him. She was killing him for nothing. She'd bring her own clan down by breaking the law, and she'd cause a rift in the magical world that might never be repaired. As he thought his final thought, as the world went dark, he mourned the failure of such a stupid and desperate plan. She'd killed him rather than saving him!

* * *

IN THE DARKNESS of death Jacob felt a presence, a gentle soul that was little more than a spark in the darkness. The blue light came near, and he sensed rather than saw, that he was nothing more than a red flame burning in the darkness. He had no form, no shape, just thoughts and flame. What had she done to him?

"You are safe, Jacob, you'll make it through the process. I know you will. You're the dragon shifter." Her words weren't really words, more the memory of sound, something he couldn't explain but he knew that he could communicate with her in this hell of nothing.

His thoughts blasted her, his rage formless as the flame that he was became a roaring inferno of grief and anger.

"What have you done to me?" When the fire had roared for what felt like hours he calmed down enough to communicate with her but it was little more than a whisper of a memory.

"You are changing. This is a phase, that's all. Only a phase. We all go through it when we're changed." Her light shifted, came nearer to his now that he wasn't flaming so high and Jacob was aware that the anger was still there but he could only be resigned to his fate for the moment.

"You're lucky you know." Her communication held a

hint of her own anger. "My maker was a cruel man, a man that created out of lust, not out of the need to enhance our species as we do now. Back then they just did it to whoever they wanted to, without even so much as a reason. I know I took you without permission, and there will be consequences, but this had to be done, Jacob. It had to be."

Her communication stopped for a moment and Jacob felt his flame go lower, his calmness making his form calm as well.

"I was born Sabrina Adelasia Giuletta Margherita Tornabuoni in the 15th century. I was distantly related to the Medici family. I lived a life of privilege, of wealth that is unimaginable, even for today's billionaires. Excess didn't even begin to cover the life we lived, even as females in that time period. It was a fairy-tale that can never be repeated on this earth. I hope it is never repeated because for all of the wealth there was sickness of the mind and body, there was unimaginable cruelty, and brutality that is only rarely seen today. We had no limits, no law to stop the things we did or schemed to have. The world was a rotten place, even if I did love my dresses and the way my hair was done, even if I did love my mother beyond all things."

So her name was Sabrina. At least he knew her name now. Little comfort as he felt a twinge of pain begin in the area where his feet should be. What was happening now? Sabrina started to communicate again and Jacob forgot the tingling pain of a thousand ants biting his non-existent toes as she spoke.

"I was married at nineteen to Giovanni Bardi, an old man from another banking family in Florence. I was grateful that he would have me at such an advanced age. He took me away from Florence, to the hills of Tuscany, when the plague came to the city. We left my family behind, my friends, anyone that could have protected me, and we fled to a small villa he owned there. I didn't like my husband but I respected him as my partner. I was heavy with our first child and I think he was more concerned about me giving birth than preserving my life." Her communications stopped and as soon as she paused the pain came back, now spreading as far as his heels and as the torture tore through him he wanted to scream.

Quickly her communications came back, easing the pain once again.

"I was having pains the night Antonio came to our door, begging for bread. If I'd known what he was really after I'd have bricked the door up to prevent what came next. I didn't know, though. I wasn't completely naïve. My father had consented to my education up until my marriage was arranged, and growing up near the Medici's you don't stay innocent for long, but I had no sense that the man was evil. Nothing jumped out at me, you know?"

The strange mix of her old world Italian, a language he had only just realized she'd been using and that he'd astonishingly understood, and modern day English drew his attention and interrupted the story.

The pain was in the back of his heels now, and the desire to scream was becoming unbearable. How did you scream without lungs?

"My pains started in earnest as I let the man in after I gave him bread and sausage to eat along with some beer, and I took to my bed. Giovanni sent for the doctor and midwife, telling them to argue it out amongst themselves over how to best treat me. I left it to the house servants to care for the man and to see him out. For whatever reason, they decided to let him stay the night. Perhaps they had discussed it with my husband, perhaps they had simply forgotten him, but he stayed."

She paused again and Jacob felt the pain crawling up his legs, legs that had not been there a moment ago. She spoke again and the pain was gone and he knew his flame was flickering with his relief. He couldn't scream but the urge to do so was there, growing stronger each time she paused.

"I labored for hours, my body fighting against me because the child wasn't turned correctly. The doctor and the midwife also argued, disagreeing over how best to save it. By the time the doctor came to me with a dirty kitchen knife to cut the child from my womb, I didn't care. I just wanted it to all be over. I was barely nineteen, newly married, newly dying."

This time his knees exploded and Jacob saw with eyes that didn't exist that her light became brighter as she came nearer, the coolness of her light dimming his own flame, somehow easing his pain.

"The child was cut from me and I heard him crying in the darkness, needing his mother, but I was too exhausted to do little more than watch my blood flow out of me. The doctor didn't bother to sew me up, he just left me to bleed to death, my duty done. My husband didn't come, and one by one the servants disappeared, until there was only my son beside me in a basket. I slipped into unconsciousness and woke up only long enough to see the man hovering over my son's basket, and then even my son was gone. And then the pain truly began. I had thought I had died but instead I was being reborn. To a world of pain, agony that is unimaginable. The pain you feel now."

For a moment, his flame grew to something that should encompass the entire globe but she came near once again to soothe him and spoke some more.

"I spent an eternity in that hell, unable to find my way out of it. When I woke up only the day had passed, no more time than that, not even eighteen hours, but my entire world had been destroyed. I found the doctor and midwife first, drained of blood, their bodies torn apart to get out even the marrow in their bones. Then my husband and the servants. I ran through the house, terrified, unaware of what I was, what I had become, but knowing only that my child was in that house somewhere. I found him in the library with Antonio."

Her flame flickered for a moment, fell in on itself as her pain increased at the memory. Jacob knew it was pain but could do little to comfort her. He was going to explode himself. Besides, she was the reason for his pain. He'd kill her if he had hands to do it with, or so he thought to himself.

Sabrina struggled but finally pulled herself together and he felt the relief her words gave him with satisfaction. Jacob wasn't sure how much more he could take. He'd felt his thighs this time and dreaded the pain the rest of him was going to feel as the change took hold of his vital organs and not just muscles, sinew, and blood vessels. He didn't think he would make it through the whole thing.

"Antonio didn't speak as I flew into the room on feet made swift by horror. The man was covered in the blood of the dead. In the blood of my servants, my husband. And he was cradling my son, the only son I would ever birth, in his arms. So when you asked me if I was trying to make some kind of hybrid child… well, I do not know. I will only ever have one child and Antonio took him from me. He sucked every last drop out my son's tiny little body and then broke him open to find every stray bit of blood he could. He did all of this as I wailed helplessly in front of him. As you will soon learn, you cannot raise your hand to your maker, you can't tell them no, and you cannot stop them from doing whatever they choose to do." Her pain flared again and Jacob knew that what he'd felt before didn't compare to the sanity-stealing pain he now felt, almost as much as hers.

"I hadn't even seen my child alive, I only saw his broken and torn body, nothing more. Lifeless, shattered, and drained of even his essence, my child was thrown at my feet, taken into my arms, and I was allowed to look on his bruised face for only a moment before Antonio dragged me away. He wanted to dress my newly healed body and take me for a night with his friends. I won't bore you with the details of the few weeks I spent with him, I will let it suffice to say that he ruined me, he ruined my reputation, and my family disowned me, though they had no idea of what I was by then. I had three weeks of absolute hell before he discarded me. I was to be grateful he taught me to fend for myself as he threw a stack of bills down at me, money to support myself until I got on my feet. I suppose that was his payment for ruining my life."

Jacob's pain when her words stopped became unbearable and he knew this must be what Hell truly was. To have your organs and body attacked by a million biting ants, ants that you couldn't brush away, or wash away, pain that was unending and unstoppable, almost cracked him. Almost.

There was a small glimmer of hope, hope that would lose consciousness once again, that the black world of nothing, where you didn't exist might return. She gave him another moment of bliss by continuing the tale, easing the pain before he went completely insane.

"I took my new clothes, my new knowledge, knowledge I'd gained, that Antonio gave with his blood the same as I give it to you, and the money I had left and I went to the Medicis. I threatened to kill them all, to wipe out the entire family line, and I could. They complied with my demands and I set out to live a life more suitable to my new status as an immortal. When people began to whisper my name too much I would move on, a new town, a new country, wait a few decades before making the rounds again. I did this endlessly for one hundred years, and though the hold of the Medicis would eventually falter, the settlement I made with them continues to support me.

In the late 18th century I found Adrian in Venice, little more than a male prostitute at the time, and turned him. I can't say that I loved him but he understood me.

As the eighth child of a nobleman he had little prospects for the future but I took him under my wing, gave him far more than he could have ever dreamed of. I gave him the world. Our affair lasted for decades, we were passionate about each other and devoted. The passion has since cooled but the devotion is still there, we still have an intimate relationship, but it is not the same as it used to be." Her communication paused and Jacob could only communicate a scream of mortal agony.

"Please, do not stop." The words were communicated with the scream and she continued, understanding fully that every time she paused his pain came back. His eyes, his brain, no he couldn't survive this, he just couldn't, not without her speaking to him, not without her taking some of the pain away. Just that small moment without her words was a lifetime of torture that no creature should ever have to endure.

"For over six hundred years I have survived. I carry the knowledge of the first hominids with me, I have an advantage that many do not. For centuries I have made my own way and have been nobody's pawn. Now your brother and the other magicals want to negotiate with the Mungons? They want to appease them or whatever it is you want to call it." Jacob could imagine her eyes rolling as she waved her hands. "No, I will not have it. These people need to be dealt with and dealt with swiftly. That is why I am creating you. I swore I would make no other vampire, other than Adrian, that he would be the only one. But we need you. We need your fire, your strength, Jacob. Do not give up. The hardest battle has not been faced yet."

And that's when Jacob exploded, when his entire being turned into little more than a firework and he shattered into orange and silver shards within the midnight darkness of the world they now inhabited. He became nothing but he knew everything. He had no form but he could create anything he wanted, centuries of knowledge passed instantly into his existence. As the light faded, so did he. There was nothing left, nothing at all.

4

Jadrian

Jadrian watched Allana as they walked to her room, her hips swaying under her green skirts in a way that drew his gaze. He wanted to know if they swiveled liked that when she was coming. Telling himself he was on a mission, not out for a good time, Jadrian entered her room and sat in the soft brown velvet chair she indicated.

"So, you're the other brother. The adopted one, right?" She said it as though he should be stung by the words but he wasn't. He knew what he was and where he fit into the scheme of things.

"I am, indeed. Human through and through, but still an Alexander." He sipped the Scotch, watching her over the rim of his glass as she walked back to retrieve her own drink.

"No resentment then? You don't feel as though they take you for granted or anything? Maybe think less of you?" She stood before him, the long material of her dress hiding the length of her legs. Was she goading him, or just too rude to hide her curiosity?

Jadrian felt his pulse begin to race as he imagined shoving the skirt up her thighs and burying his head between the parted flesh. What would she taste like? Would she taste of danger and the promise of ecstasy?

"Not a single issue there, Allana. Just devotion, the same as them." He sat back, shifting his hips to ease the tension in the front of his pants. The movement caught her gaze and a sparkle of amused curiosity came into her eyes. He took it a step further and let his middle finger fall into his glass, swilling the liquor inside with a slow swirling motion. Her eyes were glued to his fingers, watching with parted lips. She was interested then.

He'd spent hours wanting to catch her eye and now that he had it he couldn't give in, not too much anyway. No matter how desperately his body wanted to. There was something going on with this shifter.

"Oh, I think you might be very different in one aspect. Shifter men are, well, to put it delicately, endowed with certain attributes. Do you measure up?"

She sipped at her drink, teasing him by licking the last drop of the amber liquid from her lips.

His eyes followed her tongue, transfixed as his desire grew. Two could play that game but her game would lead to unknown places. She beckoned him into a world of sensuality without even trying. Shifter women were like that though, always enticing, always seductive, always fucking hot. He held himself back though, wanting her to make that first move, wanting her to be the one that broke.

"There is only one way to find out for sure. I could tell you I am just as generously endowed as any shifter but I could be lying. Perhaps I put them to shame? You'll never know…" He allowed the words to dwindle off, letting her interpret how she chose to take it.

"Mm, that sounds like an offer. Was it?" Her eyebrow arched, a slim flame above her eye, and her lips twisted into a sultry pout that he quite liked.

The tightness in his pants liked it too and he had to shift once more, the tension becoming almost unbearable. When she leaned forward and ran a finger down his cheek he felt his stomach drop and he sucked in a breath. If just her finger on his cheek felt that good, what would it feel like to have the rest of her pressed to him?

"I think I will take you up on your offer, Mr. Alexander." Soft and sensual, her words were whispered into the shell of his ear, her hot breath sending a shiver of anticipation down his spine.

His eyes went to her garment, wondering how to get it the hell off of her. But she wasn't interested in taking her own clothes off, at least not yet. It was hard to pretend he wasn't intrigued by her words when all his brain was screaming at him to do was push her far enough away to get his head between her thighs and taste her but he held himself still, his hands clenched on the arms of the chair to hold them in place.

You are only here to get into her good graces, Jadrian, he reminded himself, you do not get to fuck her. Not yet anyway.

She slithered down his chest, landing on her knees between his legs, looking up at him with a hunger he'd never seen from a woman before. With her eyes glued to his, she reached out to him, her hand going over the large ridge in his pants. Her hands were small but the size of his erection made her fingers look even smaller. Jadrian couldn't stop himself, he thrust into her hand, his body doing as it wanted, ignoring his commands.

Biting her lip she gave a murmur of delight and held back a smile. Her pale fingers ran over him as she rubbed at his hardness, teasing him through the restraining fabric.

"Shall I do something about this, now that I know you weren't just full of shit?" She brushed her hair over her shoulder, revealing the long length of her pale neck. He wanted to crush his lips to the delicate skin there, to make her shiver with delight.

"Do whatever you like, Allana. I'm not going to stop you from sucking my dick if that's what you want to do." There, he had thrown out his own challenge. It was up to her to accept or run away.

"Ah, what I'd like to do and what I'm going to do are totally different things." She didn't elaborate but opened the button and the zipper on his pants instead.

He felt the instant relief of his cock being released and gave a sigh of pleasure as the thick length escaped the confines of his pants. Jadrian wasn't sure if it was from the pleasure of the tightness disappearing or the cold feel of her fingers wrapped around the heat of his very aroused dick. Again he thrust into her hand, his hips moving of their own will, and she sighed.

He watched her, anticipating each move she made, his eyes growing wider as she leaned into him. Whatever game she was playing, she apparently enjoyed sucking dick, if that look of greedy hunger on her face was any indication. Slowly her lips parted and his muscles tensed, his eyes glued to her beautiful face as she took him into her mouth, tasting him with a moan. Her tongue darted out to test his feel and he almost came, the picture of her tongue on his dick almost too much to take.

Her mouth opened again as she winked up at him tauntingly, and Jadrian watched each inch slide in between those peach colored lips of hers, counting the seconds as she went down, down, all the way down until her nose met the wall of his abdomen. Her eyes flashed up at his and she swallowed, winking up at him as he gasped out her name.

Oh she was a dirty girl, but he loved that about her. This was no wilting damsel, this was a woman in charge of her own life, willing to kick ass and take names. But she was also willing to suck cock and make his toes curl. He might have just found the perfect woman.

She pulled away from him and he groaned as his cock slid out of her throat, out of her tight lips. He loved the way her cheeks caved in as she sucked every inch of him until he popped out of her mouth. He watched her lick her lips as she smiled up at him.

"Oh yes, you measure up just fine, cowboy." She didn't give him time to respond, she just went straight back to his cock, sucking at him with an intensity that had his toes curling in his boots.

He wanted to come, he wanted to unload all of the night's tension deep inside of her throat but the pain of just how hard he was wasn't unendurable. He held back, grinding his teeth until he couldn't take any more of it and pulled her head away.

"What's the matter?" She looked upset that he had stopped her.

Jadrian had been just on the edge of teetering into the abyss but he'd stopped her, placing his hand over his rigidly erect length, amazed at just how hard he really was. He wasn't sure he had ever been so hard, or enamored with a woman.

"Nothing, I'm not ready for this to end yet. This is not how I fuck. It's not a rush to get it over with, or a race to the finish. It's an all-night exploration of seeing just how many ways we can make each other climb the wall. It's about the experience, and about getting off in the most exquisite way possible. It's not just about fucking to me. I can fuck anytime I want to. I want more with you."

He saw her eyes flashing, curiosity filling their depths as she moved from her knees and held out his hand.

"And how do we go about that, then, Mr. Alexander?" Her body swayed as she walked to her bed, one of the larger beds the monastery offered, and climbed up on it. She tucked her feet beneath her as he stood in front of her, watching as she pulled buttons to reveal bare flesh.

He was spellbound for a moment, entirely caught up in the way she revealed her skin to him. She wasn't only beautiful, she was brave, intelligent and just on the verge of being his. He pulled his own top away, anxious to feel her warm skin against his.

"By exploring limits, my dear. By pushing until we have to stop, by pressing until the end is near, and stepping away. By making it last all night rather than just a few moments that will not matter the next day." Jadrian leaned down, taking her delicate face into the rough expanse of his hand and stroking her lip with his thumb. "We do it by taking it one step at a time, Allana."

He let his head slowly down to hers, his tongue darting out to wet his lips just before he pressed them to hers. Their breaths mingled as they both sighed at the pleasure the contact caused. Jadrian felt a pulse of heat blaze down his spine as soon as his lips touched hers, an awareness that something had just happened, but not something he could explain or define. She pulled away, gasping, as she looked at him in surprise.

He looked back, unsure of what to do next, of what had just happened but she moved, taking the decision away from him as she sat up on her knees and clasped her arms around his neck. They moved together as the kiss deepened, Jadrian took up position on the bed and Allana wrapped her legs around his waist, clasping him tight to her. Her dress hiked up around her hips and Jadrian felt her bare flesh pressing into his lower abdomen, still bare from her earlier actions. He had removed his shoes before getting onto the bed and as he felt her feet twining together at his back he knew she'd lost hers at some point as well.

They were pressed together intimately, both breathing harshly as their tongues began to tangle together. Jadrian felt her hard nipples pressing into his chest through the material of her dress and wanted to tear the material away, to have the peaks in his mouth and hands, but held back, telling himself to take it slow. Instead he teased her by running a finger over a bare hip, a movement that jolted her body as she felt the intimate brush.

Normally he had no problem with control but something about Allana made him want to completely lose it. He wanted to have her, wild and wet beneath him, open to only him, fucking him as frantically as he wanted to fuck her. Normally he didn't like sex like that but something was different, something had changed. Jadrian wasn't sure what it was but he knew it all the same.

Her breasts heaved against his chest and he finally pulled away from her mouth to inspect the mountain of cleavage peeking over the top of the dress. He used his lips to kiss the soft globes and inhaled the scent of her, an intoxicating smell, and moved his hands down to her bottom. With his hands he pressed her into him, her wetness finding his hardness, and they both moaned. She twisted in his arms, freeing her top from the confines of the material, delighting him with a corset the same color as her dress that only pushed her breasts up from the bottom without covering her nipples.

Her nipples matched her lips, a peach color, and Jadrian's gaze was glued to them. His hands pressed into her bottom again and they started a rocking rhythm, a rhythm that made her gasp as the head of his erection teased at the pleasure nub hidden between her nether lips. Each time he thrust into her she gasped, but when his lips wrapped around the bud of her nipple she made a more satisfying sound. She moaned his name.

"Jadrian." She sighed as she said it, and Jadrian felt himself grow impossibly harder.

"What, Allana?" The words were rasped against her breast, his control almost snapping.

She tossed her head back and he saw just how beautiful she was in the dawning morning light.

"What do you want? Tell me."

Allana's brows creased and she gave a mewl of dissatisfaction but he waited. She had to tell him. He needed to hear her say it.

"I want to get off, Jadrian. Get me off."

"Greedy bitch." But he laughed as he said it, a gentle sound not meant to provoke but to tease. "Just breathe and let yourself feel, just feel it. Let it consume you."

Her eyes opened, their blue depths just as startling as ever, and she looked down at him, her hips moving in time with his. "Feel your cock sliding against me? Or how your mouth pleased my nipples, dragging out pleasure I never knew existed? I do not think anyone's ever sucked them so well."

His eyes gleamed with satisfaction as she spoke. She was getting it. This wasn't just about touching, it was about feeding all of the senses.

"You're so wet, Allana, I could just breathe the right way and slide into you but you're not begging for it yet, not yet."

"Make me." Her words drug another groan out of him. He was almost ready to beg for it, even if she wasn't.

Jadrian let his lips go back to her nipples as she spoke, her arms pulling him tighter as her nails dug into his back. He groaned at the intensity of it all, releasing some of his own tension into her as his fingers dug tighter into her ass, holding her still as he began to thrust between her lips, but not into her. His fingers kneaded her ass, caressing the delicate star with her own skin, her own muscles. He hadn't planned on letting her come so quickly but the sensation must have been too much for her.

Allana cried out his name and her eyes flew open as she gasped loudly, her body tensing as the waves began to shake her. She didn't scratch him, not much, as the first flutters started to grip her. As the pulsing pleasure intensified her nails dug further into the flesh of his back, broke the skin ever so slightly, and dug just a little bit further as she rocked with the force of her ecstasy. Jadrian was fascinated as she came apart in his arms, and didn't notice the slight pain, it only added to his enjoyment as he watched her explode.

She let go completely, her hips riding him, her breast pressed into his face, her back arched in an oh-so-lovely way. Jadrian couldn't look away and didn't want to as he witnessed the magnificent woman completely lose it. He was going to sink right into her as soon as the spasms stopped, he was going to take her even higher, and he was poised for the moment, only a breath away from shifting into her, when a noise intruded. Jadrian had started to slide into her, even when the voice intruded but he knew he had to stop. He was going to murder someone.

"Alpha, you're wanted in the hall." A male voice intruded into their secret world, a world he had never wanted to leave, and Allana was gone. Jadrian felt the coldness left behind by her leaving, the emptiness she left in her wake, and looked up in confusion.

"What…" he started, but she had thrown on a robe and opened the door.

"What is it, Razor?"

Razor, Jadrian scoffed to himself, what a stupid name. He shifted on the bed, hoping she would come back.

"The Alexander Alpha can't find one of his brothers, have you seen him?" The voice stayed outside in the hallway, Allana had only cracked the door enough to stick her face through.

"Which brother? Oh never mind, I'll be out in a minute." She quietly closed the door and came back into the bedroom. "Dress yourself, your brother needs you."

Jadrian had jumped from the bed the moment his brother was mentioned and had his shirt in hand. "Do we continue this later, then?"

She paused as she threw another dress over her head, and looked at him as though he'd lost his mind. "Of course, now get out. I'll see you later."

Jadrian put his shoes and top back on and left the room, his thoughts turning to his brother but he turned before he left. "Until then, Allana."

She gave him a promise with her eyes, a promise he planned to hold her to.

It was going to be a long ass day, a very long ass day.

Jadrian left her room, his body more than a little put out with him, and went in search of his eldest brother. Something must be up for him to go to others. Was Jacob still missing?

"What's up, Cade, which one is missing this time?" Jadrian's tone was exasperated, his frustration levels higher than he had ever felt them before. Maybe it was the vampire blood but Allana got under his skin in a way he wasn't sure was normal.

"It is still Jacob and I do not sense him. I do not sense him anywhere." Cade's back had been turned to Jadrian as he typed something into his phone but now he turned haunted eyes to Jadrian.

Jadrian stepped back, the fear in Cade's eyes making his stomach drop to somewhere subterranean. He had never seen Cade with such a pained expression, not even when Kane was in an accident and had barely clung to life.

"I looked everywhere here at the complex. Has he gone back to Kansas for some reason?" Jadrian's mind was in a panic now, if Cade was that worried something was wrong. How did he calm his brother enough to keep him from falling into the same panic?

"Not that I know of, no, I would still sense him, even that far away." Cade looked closely at Jadrian for a moment, his gaze a little confused, but that cleared and he shook his head. The haunted look came back and Jadrian felt his heart breaking. He didn't like that look on his brother, any of his brothers. Especially when there was little he could do about it.

Going to his brother he grabbed his shoulder and pulled his gaze away from the phone. "We'll find him, we'll find him alive, and you will see this worry was for nothing."

Jadrian gave Cade a searching glance, looking for proof his brother believed him but didn't find any.

"I always know where you all are, always. I can't feel him at all now." Cade wiped a broad hand across his face, trying to wipe away the worry.

"I will do another search of the lower levels and outside. We'll find him. I will find him, Cade."

"Keep in contact then. I can't lose two of you." Cade already wore a defeated look and Jadrian felt like a failure for not giving his brother hope. But Cade knew things, had mad skills that only Alphas could have. Jadrian felt his stomach drop out again and his heart squeeze in panic. Where was Jacob?

Jadrian squeezed his brother's shoulder again and left the room. He tripped over his sister-in-law Damesha's dog Annie halfway down the hall, the dark passage barely lit by dim wall sconces.

"Annie, what are you doing here, girl?" Jadrian bent down to pet her. Annie was a special dog, they had all come to notice that over their time with her and Jadrian wondered.

"Have you seen Jacob, Annie? Do you know where he is?" Jadrian scratched her ears as he talked to her, and she ate the loving up.

When he stopped she looked at him with her own set of grim eyes and stood still, her body relaxed in a way that spoke of the same defeat Cade obviously felt.

"Not good then, huh?" Jadrian felt dread taking the place of the panic and pulled out his own phone, sending Jacob several texts when he didn't answer his phone. The reddish brown and white dog, medium in size, stood by his side, her Beagle-like features just as worried as his.

* * *

Jacob

"I CANNOT EASE your pain now, this part you will have to survive on your own." Her voice, in his head, all around him, eased the worst of the pain only briefly.

Whatever was happening to him had reached his eyes, his brain. The pain stole his thoughts, spun him into a world of misery unlike anything he'd experienced before. Could he endure this? He wondered in a brief moment of lucidity before the pain ate into his brain and his eyes once more. He would have screamed an eternal scream if he had been capable, but he couldn't even produce that in his state.

He heard her voice, no longer the soothing sound that eased his pain with her tale, but another annoyance. She had done this to him. If he survived, he was totally driving a stake through her heart, mistress or not. At least he assumed that is what the tale she'd told him meant. He'd be hers until she tired of him. He couldn't believe his will could be so totally subverted. He was an Alexander, no matter what form he took.

She would die the moment he could hold a dagger, a knife, or even control his hands. He'd tear her heart out with nothing more than his fingernails if he had to. Sure, she had a sad story to tell, but didn't they all? Alright, she'd been basically tortured, her brain probably snapped all those centuries ago, that would explain this completely abhorrent idea she had come up with. She'd told him she knew what it was to be taken without permission but she'd done it to him. No, Jacob decided, she had to die before she caused more chaos.

But the memory of the way she'd looked earlier; sweet, innocent, totally carnal, intruded in a moment of clarity. Her sweet beauty filled his mind and he wondered how a man, any kind of man, could have abused such loveliness. She must have been amazing as a human, full of kindness and care. The monster that he'd seen wasn't her.

Then the pain was back but it wasn't as soul-shattering. A plan was forming as the pain eased once more. He couldn't kill her, she'd only wanted to do what was best for the world. She'd only wanted love in her life, her story had told him that, but she'd never quite found it. He still wanted revenge but her death wasn't so high on his list of priorities as he finally, peacefully, came back to reality. He'd get his revenge on her in a way he knew he could truly hurt her.

Jacob opened his eyes and saw her standing over him. He stared into her eyes, his own cold with the pain he'd just endured. He would make her pay for what she'd done to him.

5

Jacob

Jacob stirred on the vampire's bed. He'd fallen into a deep sleep moments after he had regained true awareness, his first day as a vampire spent regaining his strength. He'd been vaguely aware of movement, of a soft pillow beneath his cheek, and of warmth that he'd not felt in the other place.

It had been cold there, damp, underground for sure. Almost impossible in Louisiana so perhaps she'd taken him far away? He didn't know but as he blinked slowly his gaze focused on her now familiar room. When he tried to move he found he was bound by invisible bonds. He could move on the bed but not off it.

"You'll be free to move around soon enough. You'll

be hungry, but you cannot leave until you understand what I've done." Her voice came from a corner by the fire and his head swiveled in that direction.

"Oh, I believe I understand perfectly. You want to use me as a weapon of mass destruction and destroyed me to do it." His words came out as a snarl, he'd meant to approach this differently, to stick to the plan, but his rage boiled.

"Ah, so you're not completely pliant then. I suppose that's the shifter nature coming through." She stood, moving her hair to behind her shoulders, her long dress a sapphire blue. "No matter, you'll still be bound to do as I command. The sacrifice of one for the good of many will make your hate worth it."

Sabrina moved to him, standing just out of his reach. She knew he couldn't hurt her but still stayed far enough away to be safe, he noted. Probably a wise move. Perhaps his shifter blood would do more than give him a small amount of his own will. Perhaps he'd be able to kill her after all.

He watched her as one watches a bug crawling up a wall, contemplating whether to kill it or to put it outdoors. He knew what she had planned but had no idea what exactly any of it meant. Or how he was supposed to accomplish it. He didn't particularly feel different, just not alive as he had once been. He could feel his heart beating slowly, to move the vampire blood around in his veins, he could feel a hunger building in his stomach, but he didn't feel his lungs moving as they should. Only a shallow breath was needed every few minutes.

He knew he'd been changed; the memory of the pain he had endured was too recent for him to think otherwise, the changes in his body were screaming to him that he was different, but it wasn't as bad as he had expected. Then he realized what she had just said.

"The sacrifice of one? You would rather sacrifice one when Cade didn't plan on sacrificing any? That makes your plan better?" He spoke with contempt, his eyes blasting her for a moment before he looked away, some unknown force making him bow his head.

"Not so resistant after all, I see." She chuckled and went to the fire once more. "No, Cade didn't plan on sacrificing anyone but his way leads to the sacrifice of us all. The Mungons want all of our heads on a poke, vampire, shifter, anyone else standing in their way. We have to totally destroy them. That is the only way. And this way you get some form of life, even if it's not the one you had planned on living." She sat back down in her chair, feet going beneath her. He realized he still longed for her, his desire for her hadn't changed.

Rather it seemed to have become more powerful, he realized, as his lower regions reacted to a glimpse of her cleavage. That still worked, he thought with relief.

Thank fuck for that! But to her? With a weary sigh he fell back onto the pillows. Remember the plan, Jacob, stick to the plan.

"I have to leave you, find some blood for you, but don't worry, this isn't like the movies either, we have willing donors, you just can't drink until you drain them. I will return shortly."

Sabrina stood and left the room, leaving Jacob to wonder if he'd be able to drink a human being. He didn't think he was ready for that yet.

He felt something as the minutes passed, an awareness of Sabrina. Whenever he thought about her he got a sense of where she was. A simple flash of an image, like a picture, would come into his mind, and he could hear some of her thoughts. She was worried she'd made a mistake, that taking Jacob might have been a step too far. But overriding her fear was the certainty that the Mungons were dangerous and needed to be dealt with. She'd lived for a long time, perhaps she knew better than Cade?

He pondered these new thoughts as he waited, his stance to her changing as the minutes passed. She hadn't done it because she thought she knew better. She hadn't risked a war between the magicals on a whim at all. She'd seen these kinds of enemies before, had fought in battle. Only there hadn't been a dragon shifter to save them last time, and they'd spent decades under the heel of brutal masters. All of the magicals, not just the vampires.

Jacob felt the hard edge of his rage melting as the day wore on. He knew her fears now, he knew why she has taken this chance, a chance that could bring more war to the magical world. He's the best weapon they have.

By taking him she'd joined the shifter and the vampire clans better than any marriage could have. A war between the two would be pointless, one shifter wasn't worth them all. And if what she said was true, he'd become the alpha of all of the vampires, not just of her clan. He'd be the most powerful being on earth, even above the pair sitting on the throne in the heart of the sanctuary. The enormity of it all sunk in and Jacob felt a slow panic begin. He'd been too angry to realize it before, too distraught at the change she'd forced upon him, but now he knew the fate of the world was in his rather unsteady hands.

No, he didn't have time for revenge right now, justified or not. He had to actually listen to her, hear her out, and plan. To save his brothers, his clan, and the world, he'd have to forgive for now, to let it go, and work with Sabrina. Until this was all over at least and he stood as the one true king of them all. Every last one of them.

Jadrian

JADRIAN WANDERED THE HALLS, Annie by his side, wondering where to look next. He'd searched everywhere he'd been allowed and that was every room in the sanctuary. He was tired, worried, and dreading heading back to Cade without any news. No one had seen Jacob since the day before. He'd just vanished off the face of the earth somehow!

"Well, Annie, any suggestions girl?" Jadrian looked down at the intuitive dog and followed her when she gave one of her patented head-waves.

Jadrian wasn't surprised to find she led him to the dining hall where Damesha and Kane were eating, their baby girl in a basket between them.

"There you are! I wondered where you'd been!" Damesha cried out as Annie went under the table to stand between Damesha's knees. "You've been helping Jadrian, I see. Good girl, Annie, good girl!"

Damesha obviously loved her dog and the feeling was quite mutual, Jadrian could tell, as Annie's tail started circling enough that he thought he saw her back paws come off the ground. It was the one thing that had made him smile today. Well, Allana had made him smile but that was different.

"No luck, huh?" Damesha looked guilty as she went back to eating.

"No, and don't feel guilty just because you didn't see this coming." Jadrian wagged a finger at her and took a plate from a passing waiter. He picked at the food, his hunger disappearing as he thought of Jacob. "We all know your skill doesn't work that way and none of us blame you."

She looked relieved at his words but he could see a shadow in her eyes. He knew what she was thinking, what good was the skill of having a second sight if she couldn't use it all the time? She'd been training with a professional but she'd only had a few lessons before they'd all had to come to Louisiana. It wasn't her fault but he knew she'd carry around a guilt for all of her life if something happened to Jacob. They all would.

He pushed the plate away and looked over at the couple.

"Nothing on your end either? I think I've talked with everyone." Jadrian looked over at Kane, who'd been studying him in a way that reminded him of the look he'd got from Cade earlier. "What's up, why does everybody keep staring at me like that?"

Maybe it was the vampire blood, maybe they all knew? Maybe he was too, something, anything, that would give him away?

"Something's just different about you but I can't say what." Kane, the younger version of Cade, scrunched down his right eyebrow and studied Jadrian further.

Damnit, Jadrian thought to himself. He had to stop using so much of it! "It's probably just this weird light in here."

Jadrian tried to dismiss it but Kane kept staring at him. He didn't know what could be so different, he'd been using the vampire blood for ages now. Nobody had noticed before, why now?

With more on his mind than his own appearance, Jadrian finally stood, dismissing it all. He would worry about that later, when he'd found Jacob.

"I'm going back to hunt for him, see if I can find Cade, perhaps he's heard something." He leaned over to peck Damesha on her dark cheek, then shook his brother's hand, clasping it to his chest for a moment. "We'll find him."

They had to, they couldn't give up. Jacob was a part of their unit, they couldn't have lost him. Not now when they were all needed the most!

6

James Elliot

"**M**r. Elliot, dinner is ready." The quiet voice of his servant, a man dressed in motorcycle boots, leather pants, and a leather jacket, seemed out of place in the cabin in the swamp they now inhabited. The Alexander brothers had done a number on his clan but they hadn't discovered the large house sitting in the middle of a Cajun suburb deep down a bayou road.

They were hiding in plain sight and so far it had worked. His members were currently spread across Louisiana, Kansas, Texas, and Alabama but they could all be called back quickly enough. He kept only his most trusted men with him, and a few women, of course.

He winked at one named Sherry and waved his hand

at the door to the dining room. What might seem like little more than a cabin to James Elliot would be a mansion to others. Made from cypress wood, the house was three stories tall and surrounded in glass. Decorated by a professional, the house wasn't to the man's style but appealed to the ladies with lots of magnolia flower motifs and *fleur de lys* patterns on almost everything.

"Ah, Sherry, you're my favorite, my dear." He slipped an arm around her waist as she came up to him, her eyes already working on seduction. They made a handsome couple, she with curly, dark red hair, a slim waist with large hips and breasts that appealed. In a slinky electric blue dress, she looked fantastic and she knew it. The man beside of her was as equally blessed in the looks department. Tall, handsome, with black hair and gray eyes James would have been a work of art, except for the cruel twist of his mouth that was always there and the greed that burned in his eyes. Those two features took away every bit of handsome about the man. Not even the tame outfit of a pale yellow buttoned shirt with a pair of khaki pants could make him appear sweeter, not with the cruelty so imprinted on his face.

James walked into the dining room with Sherry at his side. His generals were already at the table, quietly waiting for him. Clan heads, these men were powerful and in his pocket. They sat quietly as he flirted with Sherry by putting her in her chair, ignoring their hungry bellies. He could hear their stomachs and prolonged his discussion with her by sitting at the head of the table and carrying on his conversation.

"Well, you know my dear, once we rid ourselves of these pesky Alexanders and whoever else has joined with them, I'll be glad to get you a house in Hawaii. I'll name it after his parents. Do you know they pined away for each other, only twenty-five feet apart?" He asked with a cruel laugh. "I watched them wither away for weeks, unable to even see each other. That was love, true love. But yes, I'll buy you a house, my dear."

She tittered as he patted her hand, her cheeks blushing prettily but he knew in a matter of hours she'd be beneath him, getting him off in any way he imagined. And he had a very vivid imagination.

"Now, men, let's eat." He looked around the table with a wide grin, ignoring the sighs of relief. He was hungry tonight as well; he wouldn't make them wait for their meals any longer.

James gave the servant the signal and the food was brought out to the table. James parceled it out, giving the most to those who'd been the most helpful and leaving little for those that thought being a part of the Mungons Clan meant sitting on their ass while everyone else worked. It was a recent trend and one he meant to squash.

"Now men, I know you'll look at these portions and

think them unfair but you get what you earn with me. If we want to restore the king to the throne, if we want to do away with that prissy little court the magicals now call our governing body, we all have to work equally, and harder than ever."

James looked around and saw his generals watching him, focused on nothing more than him and his words. He had them in the palm of his hand. It was his cruelty that had drawn them but they had never expected him to use it on them. Now they were learning differently.

"Alpha, we shall strive to work harder!" This from a blond man to his right, one with a bigger plate of food. The man looked pleased with himself for having achieved more than he could eat. James wasn't sure he liked that. With narrowed eyes he looked at the man, wondering if he'd been wrong about him. Perhaps the man had too much ambition.

"I'm sure you will. You'll set a good example for the others." James continued to pass out food, his voice dismissive of the man and his words.

"Now, what have you all accomplished today?" James already knew every move the generals made but he wanted to hear it from them.

"I contacted my people in Louisiana. I have learned the Alexanders are all there, every last one of them." The man, another blonde, spoke with pride as though he had brought his Alpha vital information.

"We already knew that." James glared at him, scraping some of the food from the plate he had been preparing.

"But we didn't know the wives were there too!" The man's eyes had gone round and his voice got higher as he watched his food disappearing.

"In fact we did. Your information is of no use. What else did you do?" James stood, spoon in hand as the man thought. "That's what I thought. Do more tomorrow and you'll get proper food."

James handed the man a plate with two sprouts and a tiny sliver of ham, barely enough to even get the taste in his mouth. The men could go out and get their own food, James knew that, but this was a lesson in consequences. It was a lesson in standing up and being counted by your peers, not just sitting on your ass and waiting on others to do your work for you. Even generals earned their keep around here.

"Another day of this, Elias, and I'll send you to West Virginia, understand me?" James stared down at the now blanching man. James sent the worst of his people to West Virginia, the ones that refused to work, that would not even provide for themselves. They lived in squalor, deep in a mine where guards kept them from escaping. "How old are you Elias?"

"I will be thirty-two next month, Alpha." The man

swallowed harshly and James knew he had him thinking.

"So nearly three hundred years down a mine doesn't sound too pleasant, does it? I've heard some shifters live to four hundred, you know? That's an awfully long time." James's voice had become harsher as he spoke until anger blazed from his eyes.

"Yes, Alpha. I understand, Alpha." The man hung his head, not touching his food.

"Eat what you've been given. At least show that much respect for your brothers and your Alpha." James spit the words out, his fist coming down on the table.

Elias swallowed pitifully and picked up his fork. James sat down and turned off his anger, turning happy eyes to the others.

"Now, who's next?" He began to eat as the others began to speak.

As they waited for dessert, James began to speak again.

"I know I shouldn't have to go over this again but let me explain to you all what's happening here. To make sure you all understand. A refresher course for Elias, if you will. The magicals' last king died a hundred years ago and the people decided that they wanted elected officials from each branch of the world, even if some of those officials were truly shadow officials. And I do mean shadows." James stopped, rolling his eyes. "Shadows as elected officials. Only in our world!"

"We'll soon sort that, Alpha, you'll be our true and rightful king!" The first blond general crowed, James couldn't remember his name at the moment.

"Yes, well. That will only be the case if we all work for it, men. Only then!" James looked at each one, willing them to bow their heads to him. They all did.

This would work out fine then.

"While you've all been out gathering old news, others have been building tunnels. The time has come to use those tunnels, to destroy the Alexanders, to destroy those that would stand in our way!" James roared the last to the delight of his men. "Tonight we go to Louisiana. We start the process of ridding ourselves of those that have withheld power from us. We take some of that control they hold so close to themselves, and we begin our efforts."

"We shall rule the world, Alpha!" A general at the end of the table chirped up, a sycophantic man that didn't deserve a higher place, not even Elias's place.

James looked at him and began the next part of his speech. "Some of you will be lost but your sacrifice will not be in vain."

The man blanched, the meaning not lost on him. James gave him his evil grin, a grin that meant he'd fucked up royally.

"Some of you will be pawns, while others will rise to the top with me. After tonight, we don't get to rest. We have to destroy those that would hold us back. We have to decide who lives and who dies. The vampires will have to be spared for their blood. If we want to rule the world we need slaves, and the humans we leave and allow to breed will be controlled by the vampire blood. The other shifters, though?" James paused, pretending to consider the matter. "Kill them all. Every last one of them."

A cheer went around the table as James flipped his hand. Turning to Sherry he ignored the pleased sounds the men made and focused on the woman. James had a secret, he was far older than any of the current magicals suspected, he was of the first line, the oldest magical on the planet. But Sherry didn't need to know that when he took her to his bed and his men didn't either. They just needed to know their leader was strong, virile, and ready for battle. Even if he did look a bit of a tit in his outfit. The power was still there, throbbing under the surface and they all knew it.

He'd waited for this moment for an eternity, now it was almost in his hands.

7

Jacob

Jacob had recovered his senses enough to move around and explore. Occasionally an odd, stray thought would pop into his head, stopping him as he wondered where it came from. After a rather strange thought, the idea that he really hated bone-ribbing in corsets, he knew the thoughts were Sabrina's and not his own. Good to know.

Jacob wasn't sure what he was looking for as he went through the closet in Sabrina's room, he was just filling time more than anything, trying to avoid the mirror. He knew the legends, he knew vampires were doomed never to see their own reflection again and he didn't want to face it. Not that he was vain, it was the fact that even more than the ties he now had with Sabrina, or the fact that his hair had grown down to his shoulders since his "rebirth", or even the fact that his skin was much paler than it used to be, not being able to see his own reflection would mean he really had changed and life would never be the same.

He had explored every part of her room except her dressing table, the table with the mirror. With a sigh he walked over to it, avoiding the reflective surface as he came up to the side. A round silver box sat on the table and he picked it up. There was a brownish white powder in it but Jacob didn't know what it was. Holding it up to his nose he sniffed delicately.

Immediately a stinging sensation started in his nostrils, and he held the box away as he felt an explosive sneeze coming on. Jacob almost dropped the box as his reflexes took over and his fangs came down hard on his lips.

"What the hell?" He put the box down and stroked his lip. His fingers came away with blood. "Oh this fucking sucks! I can't even control my fangs? Wait, fuck, I have fangs!"

Jacob probed his gums with his index finger, finding the fangs had retracted as he searched his mouth. How did he get them to come out? He couldn't go around sniffing pepper boxes every time he needed to... feed.

Why did she have pepper in her room anyway, he wondered, as he looked down at the table again. He saw another box with salt in it, the top clear glass. Maybe she ate in her room a lot? He looked more closely at the boxes and realized they were quite old; some of the edges used to be sharp but had smoothed down over time. Perhaps it was something from her mortal life?

He put the box down and sighed. He couldn't put it off any longer. With a deep breath he moved, eyes glued to the glass mirror on the stand, waiting, hoping. Five minutes later, after scrubbing at his eyes with his fingers, after shifting around from side to side, tilting the mirror several times, and wiping it with a towel he found, he had to admit it. He had no reflection. For all intents and purposes, he didn't exist according to the mirror.

Jacob backed up, his knees coming into contact with the bed. With a huff he let himself fall onto it, his heart racing. Well, his heart was still beating, that was a plus. He had never understood the need for blood if the heart wasn't beating, as so many books and movies had claimed. It would just sit there, coagulating in the throat if none of the normal bodily functions were taking place. Yet, he couldn't see his reflection, what scientific reason could there be for that?

Even as a so called "magical", Jacob had always looked for scientific explanations for mysteries but couldn't think of an explanation as to why he didn't cast a reflection. There was just no logical reason. He was working himself into a panic, he knew that, but couldn't stop it. Find Cade, his brain screamed, but he knew that was the last fucking thing he should do. Cade would bring the entire monastery down around his ears if there wasn't a buffer there.

Jacob stood on shaky legs, his body exhausted but his mind still reeling, and felt a cry of anger and frustration building in his throat. This just wasn't good enough.

"I'm here, Jacob. And I've brought what you need most. Now settle down." Sabrina's voice came after the slight snick of the door opening, her voice soothing him, though he didn't really want to feel that way towards her.

Jacob couldn't stop his head from turning in her direction, her presence drawing him in a way he'd never experienced before.

"What do you mean..." His words trailed off as he saw a woman step out from behind Sabrina. Jacob inspected the petite blonde woman, noting her almond shaped eyes and slender frame. His eyes showed no interest until he looked back at Sabrina. His heart sped up when he saw her amused gaze, the color of her eyes somehow deeper, richer than before. Perhaps it was the sunlight, he mused as he settled back onto the bed once more.

"What's this?" Nonchalant, almost zero real interest.

"This, for lack of a better term, is dinner. Now, let

me explain a few things." Sabrina gestured to the woman to sit beside Jacob on the bed, her skirt swishing around her feet. The woman did like to dress the part, he noted, as he inspected the red crushed silk with black lace trim. Beautiful, sexy, and elegant, Sabrina was a dream come true for some, a waking, tormenting nightmare for Jacob. Mainly because he wanted her still, despite what she had done to him.

"First, no rape. I do not expect such things from an Alexander but we vampires have learned it must be stated. Taking blood can be highly erotic, arousing the deepest of passions, but rape is simply not condoned. Most of your volunteers will not mind having sex with you if you ask, most find it a highly enjoyable experience, but you must ask. Second, do not abuse your volunteer. No bruising, no pain, unless they ask for it of course." Sabrina stopped to wink at the blonde woman next to Jacob. The only thing he really noticed about the woman was that she exuded a rather pleasant perfume, something that caught his imagination.

"Jacob? Are you paying attention?" She waited until he'd turned back to her, her amused look increasing. It drove him mad! "Third, your instincts will guide you but I will be present the first few times you feed in case you need help. For some, this can be a difficult stage to face. The mind shrinks at the thought of drinking blood but you're already catching that scent are you not? At first it reminds you of spring renewal, orange blossoms and sunshine. Then it will change, have you noticed yet?" She paused, coming to him as he leaned almost imperceptibly towards the blond woman.

"She smells of chocolate and wine now, of sweet cream and butterscotch." Sabrina moved close to the bed, her eyes mesmerizing Jacob. She reached out, flicked something, and soft music with a deep bass beat started to play. When she spoke again her voice was just as soft and sensual, her words causing something in him to ache.

"Stroke her neck, Jacob. Look how long, pale and slender it is. That's it, touch her, feel her warmth." Sabrina came up on the other side of Jacob and all three sprawled on the bed, sideways on the extra-large mattress. Jacob reached out to touch the woman, a long powerful finger stroking her delicate ivory skin hesitantly. She wasn't dinner, no matter what he did to her. This was a human being, even if she wasn't as engrossing as Sabrina. He leaned into the volunteer, and to his surprise found she did smell of chocolates and wine.

Deep inside, a fire still burned, a rage he harbored against Sabrina, the woman that had changed him but might have saved the entire world. He felt no real desire for the woman but something did yearn for what she could give him. The scent did make him long for something… more.

His hands stroked the woman's neck and wandered down her shoulder, her warmth just as inviting as the smell of the blood she offered him. He jerked slightly when he felt Sabrina touch him, her small hand cold, but not as cold as he might have expected. Jacob felt a heat begin to build just beneath his skin, a skimming of fire that went straight to one place as Sabrina's hands glided over his back. The fire skimmed down, low and heavy in his lower regions. This almost felt like lust, he realized.

"Lick her, Jacob, while you're stroking her arm, lick the pulse in her neck." Sabrina whispered in his ear, so low the woman wouldn't hear, but he saw the woman tense in anticipation, her trusting eyes darting to Jacob's.

Why did she trust him, he wondered? He wasn't sure he trusted himself at this point.

Slowly, with a shyness he'd never felt before, he moved his lips to the woman's neck, tasting her with his lips. She tasted of heaven and all of the things Sabrina had described! His tongue came out then, greedily wanting more. He inhaled deeply as he tasted her, filling his head with the aroma of this rather brave woman. Or was she stupid? Jacob had no idea and didn't care as his lust for her blood burst suddenly into life. His fangs sprang from his gums, grazing her skin, and she groaned with anticipation of pleasure.

He gathered her to him as Sabrina moved, sitting up behind him to slide her hands around to his front, finding him hard and ready in more ways than one. He felt her small hand palming his hardness as his fangs slid out further from his gums and straight into the woman's flesh.

"Higher Jacob, just a little higher." Sabrina's croon told him where to go, what to do, as his needle sharp fangs slid out of the woman's skin and moved higher. He felt Sabrina squeeze him just a little tighter as his fangs slid into a new patch of skin, unbroken and paper thin, at least to his teeth. He thrust into Sabrina's hand again, wanting to feel her slick walls around him once more. "There, my darling, now suck."

He did and the most beautiful liquid he had ever tasted filled his mouth, his senses, his entire being with pleasure. He was unaware of his hands roaming the volunteer's body, or how she moaned and writhed beneath him. He was only aware of the gentle, healing pleasure of her blood as he sucked small doses of it from her slowly.

"That's it, my darling. Slow, gentle, make her feel how much you love this, make her feel a fraction of what she is giving you." Sabrina's hands had slid beneath his pants, popping the buttons that held it closed, to take him out and stroke him as he fed, but now she poured a liquid into her hand, something slick and warm, before going back to him, his legs bare from kicking the pants away.

The woman, probably in her mid-twenties, continued to move beneath Jacob, her hand guiding his to her breast to stroke a nipple, then lower, to slide her short black skirt up, and he found her bare, waiting for his touch. Jacob's first initial rush of pleasure had only grown but he became aware now that he wasn't alone, that Sabrina was touching him most intimately, that he was thrusting into her tiny little hand, and that his own hand was buried in the wet hot folds of his blood volunteer.

Where he had felt no sexual impulse he now wanted nothing more than to have one of these women riding him, fucking him, until he exploded inside of them. But he held back, too new to make demands, no matter how badly his dick wanted to be in one of them. Especially Sabrina.

His fingers, stumbling with confusion for a moment, regained their skill as he focused on the women surrounding him, one in front, one behind, one touching him, the other being touched. He stroked his fingers through the woman's wet, heated folds as his lips sucked at her flesh, stopping for a moment to suck at the nipple she had left exposed.

With an exploratory dip, he found her depths wet and ready for more, for him. She wanted him, and in that moment he wanted her. His eyes opened for a moment, staring at the blonde woman, before glancing down. He saw tiny, circular scars there and knew, just knew this had to be a favorite of hers.

She liked pain with her pleasure, he saw, and decided to give it to her. She could obviously play rough, but not too rough. He brushed at the pale pink bud of her nipple with his nose, circling it as his fingers circled her clitoris, drawing her to a higher plane as his teeth pierced the skin of her nipple.

She started to shake as he drew blood from her, a low guttural sound gasping from her throat as her back arched. Jacob watched her, his own body reacting to her, to the pleasure now making her blood even sweeter. As she came apart the taste of her became headier, filled him more deeply, and Sabrina began to speak again.

"Do you want to be inside of her, Jacob, filling her as she clenches around you? You can, if you but ask. You'll have to let loose of her nipple but I can take your place there. Or I can keep stroking you, I quite like doing it, you know? You are so big, after all! I'd heard you Alexanders were well endowed but my, oh my!" Her tongue flashed out, licking the shell of his ear, and Jacob felt his own shiver, awareness of Sabrina now making him harder, more aroused, if that were possible.

Jacob wasn't sure how it was possible but he felt it, he felt her hand around his dick, he felt it as she stroked him, felt how impossibly fucking hard he was, and knew that if he fucked either of them it would have to be Sabrina because only she could handle what he had to give. The delicate creature in front of him would break if he tried to fuck her the way he wanted to fuck the demoness behind him.

But yes, he did want to be inside of her, the small blond with the cute tits, her bare pussy tight and wet in his hand. He slid two of his fingers into her as she breathed a sigh of relief, her sigh turning to surprise, and then excitement. Vampires could fuck all night, after all. Would he fuck her, he wondered. He wanted to watch her get off once more, see how much she could take, before he fucked her.

His lips sucked at her nipple harder, his eyes scanning her body to see that the green-eyed doll Sabrina had brought him apparently liked to play rough. Thin scars covered her abdomen and Jacob caught glimpses of her memories as he fed from her now, staring at the scars. The woman enjoyed games much darker than he'd ever be willing to play, but he knew he could give her some of what she needed, he just couldn't abuse a woman in such ways, even if she did ask for it.

He was all for pleasure, a good time, pushing boundaries, but fucking that left scars like that, scars that weren't from scratches of intense pleasure, nope, those games weren't for him. But, he liked Sabrina's words, the dirty way she spoke to him, the way she was still stroking him, making this a mind-blowing experience rather than the dreaded one she'd described. He'd not been looking forward to this part but now, well now he almost couldn't wait for the next time and he wasn't even done with this time yet.

A sound at the door made the trio shift as Adrian came in. The other vampire looked at the trio and began to undress.

"Are you done with her, Jacob? Collette is a most tasty morsel and I haven't seen her in a while, if you don't mind?" The handsome man gestured to the chaise lounge and the woman, Collette, went to him, jumping up to wrap her legs around Adrian's waist. Adrian had spoken in a precise manner, a controlled way that Jacob hadn't heard from him before. Apparently Adrian was a chameleon, changing with the environment.

"No, I don't mind at all." Jacob fell back to the bed, his fangs tucked away but his dick still hard in Sabrina's hand. He turned to her, her blue eyes still amused but aware, her nostrils flared with desire, and he thrust into her hand once more as he wrapped his own hand around hers. "I would prefer fucking Sabrina anyway. She seems to like my dick well enough."

He dared her, challenged her, but he wasn't sure why. Something about her drove him to a kind of madness, a place where he acted out of character and did things he wouldn't normally do. Like fucking the woman that had destroyed him, the woman who'd given him everything. His black eyes, shiny in the darkened room, stalked her as she moved towards him, her hand coming out to stroke the hair that had grown down to his shoulders sometime during his ordeal.

"You hate me now, Jacob, I understand, it's only reasonable. I didn't ask you after all, I just took you. But I didn't do it for selfish reasons, or to hurt you personally. Please forgive the unforgivable." Her eyes, so blue, pleaded with him and Jacob felt the rage inside dim a bit more, the flame of his hatred waning just a bit.

"I can only do what I can, Sabrina, no more." His words were strangled, forced out of a throat gone tight with emotion. He wasn't used to feeling this much, to wanting and hating someone so intensely at the same time. His conflicting emotions were wearing him out and finally, he decided to do what he always did, do what was necessary for the good of his family, for his brothers, but also for himself.

Because if he didn't soon get his dick in her he'd be over there throwing Adrian off of Collette to fuck her instead. Somehow, Jacob knew the other woman wouldn't satisfy him, not the way Sabrina could. With a sigh of resignation, Jacob fell back against the bed once more, his pants disappearing as he pushed them away. He wanted her, there was no denying that, and now, after the ordeal of a lifetime, he was going to have her. He had no plans of forming a bond with her, of falling in love, or being her consort, he was an Alexander, but for tonight he was going to fuck her, and let her think as she pleased. Fuck what was right and wrong, he decided, at least as far as his own feelings went, he'd fuck her and keep her happy, and see where this took him. It might save his brothers, after all.

Jacob could hear Collette and Adrian across the room and looked over to the see the tiny vampire groupie, no taller than five feet, was astride Adrian, her back arched as she found a pace she liked. Jacob looked back over at Sabrina and raised an eyebrow.

"Sometimes it's fun to not be alone, you know? Adrian and I have been together for a long time now, it's not so shocking for us. You've been through an experience that's shattered many before you. We can find privacy if you'd like but I have a feeling you may need her again before the night is over. We don't take much at a time, but in our new stages we must feed frequently. Collette will be fine if you don't get too greedy. Besides, I love hearing her as she comes, it makes me feel so, hmmm, delicious."

"She is rather lovely, but she is not as beautiful as you." Jacob ventured a compliment, one he meant, and saw it pleased her.

"I suppose I am, but it's how you use it, is it not? If

you use it for your own gain you never really get far, but when you use it to please others…" Her words trailed off as she moved over Jacob, settling between his legs as she came up to kiss him. Her captivating eyes held him spellbound as her black eyebrows arched, their softness too enticing not to touch.

"How can even your eyebrows be beautiful?" He wondered aloud as he stroked the silky hair, their arch just right to make her appeal intense.

"Good genes, lots of practice? The vampire blood? Very few of us are unappealing but I think that's because we only make those we desire." Her words, spoken into his ear, let Jacob know her choice had not been made solely for practicalities' sake. She had desired him.

"You Alexanders are a gorgeous lot, but you, Jacob, always in the shadows when you should be in the light. You tempted me." Her fingers trailed down his face, over his lips, down to the flat plane of his stomach. She flattened her hand out there, pushing her fingers down to his hardness, to grasp him in her small palm.

Jacob stood over six feet tall, most people were tiny to him, and Sabrina, born in an age when nutrition wasn't mapped out by the government, was still lucky enough to be taller than average. She must have seemed a veritable giant in her time, but coming from a wealthy family her diet would have been better. At over five-and-a-half-feet tall she was average for the women of today but still shorter, smaller, far more delicate looking than him.

"Kiss me, Sabrina." He'd never asked a woman to do that before but there was a streak of the romantic in Sabrina, something about her that made him want to return it.

Her lips pressed into his, her blue eyes closing as her face neared his, and he inhaled her taste, sweet juicy peaches. He loved it.

She opened to him with a moan, her tongue coming out to tempt his to play. He followed her lead, twisting his own tongue with hers as her hand began to stroke his cock, softly, with ease, until he moaned into her mouth, his head falling back as pleasure took him once more. He wanted to bury himself in her, to watch her as she rode him, her breasts swaying with her motions. Opening his eyes, he saw Collette and Adrian had moved. Collette was on her hands and knees facing Sabrina, her full breasts bouncing as Adrian slid into her.

"Are you sure you don't want her, Jacob? I can call her back." Sabrina brought his face back to her and he shook his head.

"No, just you. All I need is you." He wouldn't have admitted it but his brain and voice went to work without his consent.

"Then you shall have me." She shifted, straddling his

hips with a swiftness he had never seen in a human woman, and her thighs embraced his hips.

Jacob stopped breathing altogether for a moment as he waited, watching the woman who could have filled his dreams lower herself to his cock. He wanted to see it all, his cock disappearing inside of her, the way her face changed as she felt him opening her slit, the way she arched her back as she grew used to his size, a size most women found daunting. His eyes moved from place to place, his body reacting to her, to her touch. When she slid down onto him, his skin tightened, delighting in the wet way she enclosed him in her heat.

When he slid into her slowly but easily, without a struggle, he knew he had a woman that could handle what he had to offer, and thrust up into her, making her back arch even more. Jacob felt his balls pull up close to his body and told himself to relax, to let her have her way with him. He wanted nothing more than to flip her over and pound her until he lost himself in her but he held himself back.

Each thrust became harder to control as she slid up and down his length, her hands clenching at his thighs behind her. Her face was a mask of concentration as she found just the right rhythm with his thrusts, and began a pace no human could keep up with.

Collette must have been watching them or she was

getting off again because Jacob heard her cries join Sabrina's. Sabrina looked down at Jacob and smiled.

"She is so hot for it, always is. Maybe later we will play with her again."

"Bit of a bad girl, are you?" Jacob asked with cool amusement.

"Not really, I've just lived too long not to explore the pleasures life has to offer. She is one of them, as are you." With that she flipped them, the instant change shocking Jacob for a moment.

"You'll have to teach me that later," he said, pulling up her left leg to flex into her, his dick pounding into her, stretching her until she was gasping his name, her control gone. Jacob felt a deep satisfaction when her walls clamped down around him and she began to keen out his name.

With a sensual serpentine motion, he stroked into Sabrina, his body aching for release but wanting her to finish. He wanted her pleasure, he needed it because it fed his own, and made him even fucking harder.

Jacob felt her teeth biting into his shoulder as he plunged into her, and realized he'd pulled them up so that she now sat in his lap, his dick deep inside her as she continued to explode around him. He felt the moment of pain and enjoyed it, letting her take his newly replenished blood. As she drew on his skin he felt his control slip until he was plunging into something unlike anything he'd felt in his life.

His balls shot out their cream, filling her, but it went on much longer than normal. It was harder, more powerful, almost painful, but the good kind of pain. As he gave her his load he felt his brain go to a new place, a place where nothing existed but exquisite pleasure and the peach scent of Sabrina. He lost himself in that place for what felt like hours, until reality intruded once more, taking the peace away.

She was slumped in his arms, her arms around his waist, her long hair tangled between them. He gulped in air, trying to settle his frantically beating heart. Where had she sent him to? What had she done to him? He knew the part about being a vampire but something had shifted inside his soul and suddenly she was bound to him in a way far different than before.

He pulled back a little to look down at her, and saw her looking up at him with wide eyes. Her ruby lips were parted in a slight "O" and he knew she'd felt something different as well. He felt something spasm through him again and her eyes went even wider.

"Your eyes just went wider." Her words were quiet, softly spoken and awestruck.

"Did they go red?" They did that sometimes when he shifted and came back to his human form.

"Kind of. More orange than red. Is that your shifter side?" She sounded puzzled.

"Yep, you might have just done more than you think, Sabrina. You might have just created two shifter-vampire hybrids, not just one." He didn't tell her the part about the soul-mating. He had to keep that to himself for now, until he was sure. Until he knew it wouldn't be used against him.

He brought Sabrina down on the bed, the other pair quiet now as well, and pulled the covers over them. Forced into being a vampire and soul-mated in the same damned week. What the fuck else was this week going to bring him?

Tired, confused and wanting nothing more than for the world to make sense again, Jacob closed his eyes, dreading seeing his brother later. Cade was definitely going to lose his shit.

8

Jadrian

Jadrian, exhausted and discouraged, walked back to his room pondering whether to use the rest of the vampire blood he had or try and get a few hours of sleep to quench the soul-draining exhaustion making his feet drag. He'd watched from his phone as the clan members left at their home in Kansas tore apart the houses and grounds of the many homes they owned there, no sign of Jacob being found. When technology failed to uncover his brother's whereabouts he'd gone back to searching around New Orleans, driving the straight streets, dodging tourists that wandered out into the streets as though it were part of the sidewalk.

He'd given several a good view of his middle finger

when they'd shouted at him for using the street as it was meant to be used. He didn't have the time or the patience for dealing with idiots. Throwing open his door with a growl, he went to the cabinet where he'd hidden the remaining vials, something telling him that the blood was going to be vital. They were in battle mode with the Mungons. Not one person had said the words out loud, but Jadrian couldn't help but think them now: Jacob had been taken by the Mungons.

It was the only explanation that made sense. Punctual, always cooperative, sensible, and far too concerned with his brothers, Jacob wouldn't have just taken off without an explanation of some kind. Something had happened to him and that something had to involve those bastards trying to ruin it for everybody. Selfish pricks only cared about themselves, Jadrian thought, as he tossed back the somehow still warm liquid.

Swallowing without tasting, he put the vial in the trash and stretched out on his bed, knowing the effects would start almost immediately, but still tired. He felt the scratches on his back, tiny little things that shouldn't bother him a bit, begin to itch as he settled into the pillows, his fingers going to scratch the small tears in his skin. An infection from scurrying around the dirty confines of the monastery was the last thing he needed.

They reminded him of Allana, and the reason he was itching now. His overactive imagination played an image of her on her knees, his cock sliding between those pouty lips of hers, her eyes wide. Jadrian's stomach tightened and his hands clenched the bedcovers. Shit, she was so fucking hot! If there were any gods they should let him find out what it really felt like to have her, in every way.

"Jadrian! Open up! Hurry!" An urgent voice and a fist pounding on his door startled him from his reverie and Jadrian pulled his hand from his hip where it had been snaking down.

With the swiftness only vampire blood could give him, Jadrian flew at the door, pulling it nearly from its hinges as his powerful arms flung the barrier open. Something was wrong, Cade sounded panicked.

"Is it Jacob?" Jadrian's face showed his terror as he looked up at his brother's face, the moment freezing his heart in his chest.

"No, it is the Mungons. They have built tunnels underneath the monastery, they're coming in. Damesha saw them." Cade turned, and Jadrian followed.

Damesha, their sister-in-law, was psychic and sometimes saw flashes of things that were happening out of her view or were about to happen. Jadrian followed his brother as they stalked to another part of the building, a group of people already gathered around a doorway. Cade walked between the crowd, going to the door where Allana stood. She spoke as Cade came to stand by her side.

"Right, we're evacuating most of the building. If you're not a fighter and do not want to go down in these tunnels, you have to leave with the others. We're sending those people to safe-houses in Mississippi and to Cade's place in Kansas. We suggest you go, staying here is not an option. What's coming up those tunnels is ruthless, without sympathy, and without any kind of human kindness. If you stay, be prepared to fight to the death because death is coming for somebody today."

Allana was beautiful in a black leather two-piece outfit that covered her arms and legs, her face fierce and determined. Beauty personified. As Jadrian watched her, taking in her words, he felt the renewing surge of the vampire blood in his veins. He felt invincible! As the crowd began to roar around him, Jadrian joined in, his fist going in the air. He'd follow her to Hell and back!

People began to pour out to a section of the monastery kept as an armory or to buses outside, each taking their own chosen path. Jadrian followed Cade, his blood still singing, and picked up several knives, a small 9 mm pistol, and a long iron staff. It matched his height and he thought it could serve several purposes.

"I have sent Jacqui, Damesha, the baby, and Kane to the main house in Kansas. This isn't going to be pretty. Damesha saw a lot of death, on all sides, before Kane said she passed out. Are you ready for this, brother?" Cade looked down at his brother and for a moment the chaos disappeared and Jadrian could only see his brother's eyes. The eyes of his Alpha, shifter eyes blazing with an orange glow.

"My life for you brother, for all of us," Jadrian swore as he held his arm up to his brother.

Cade grunted and clasped Jadrian's arm.

"My life for yours, Jadrian. Always." Cade's eyes flashed once more and he let his brother go. "Keep an eye out, many of us will likely shift so watch out for our family amongst the crowd of others. This could get ugly in an instant."

"I will, Cade. I'll be right behind you." Jadrian's voice shook but not with fear, his anger was boiling. These bastards had been fucking around for months and now they wanted to destroy them all. Not on his watch.

Jadrian snuck down to the cellar with Cade and the rest of the magicals, at the head with Allana and Cade.

"Which way?" Allana whispered back to Cade, their eyes able to see in the darkness, but Jadrian didn't have that ability. He strained to see but couldn't.

"Down to the end, then to the right, there's a hole in the floor." Damesha had paid attention, Jadrian noted.

In single file the crowd made it to the room, shifting as they entered. Jadrian tried to memorize specific markings, noting that Allana shifted to a beautiful tiger with black marks around her eyes. Cade shifted into a black jaguar, a blonde shape over his green eyes. Jadrian knew that was a manifestation of his bonding with Jacqui. They were ready but he felt a tremor of uncertainty for a moment. He wasn't a shifter after all.

Stealing his nerves, he jumped with his brother into the dank darkness, his feet making a noise as he slid in the mud. Cade made a sound and Jadrian stopped, he would give them all away with his boots. He felt something soft and silky brush his hand and somehow knew it was Allana. He tangled his fingers in her fur and they stayed at the back of the line, waiting for their cue.

Instinctively, Jadrian knew he needed to stay at the back until he was needed. A loud roar came through the darkness, a sound filled with surprise and rage, and Jadrian heard the sound of shots being fired, of knives meeting metal, and he ran through the tunnel, fighting for clearance to find Cade. A glow started as he ran, and light soon chased away the darkness. He found Cade with Allana by his side and plunged a knife down into the back of a wolf squaring up to his brother. The blade sank deep but Jadrian pulled it free easily, turning away from the dead creature to seek a new foe.

Allana had a coyote by the throat, shaking it like a rag doll before she threw the broken body on the floor. People were engaged in hand to hand combat now, the tide of Mungons never-ending. Jadrian kept back in a passage, Allana right beside him, as a wave of bears came at him with faces snarled into fierce rage.

He brought the iron shaft around, backing up further into the tunnel, totally unsure if he and Allana could take them all on. She finally stood her ground, letting out a roar as the group of bears shrank away from her suddenly, turning to run the other way. Letting out another roar she stalked to the end of the tunnel, Jadrian following her. He could see his brother standing with a group of their clan members, looking confused as the Mungons retreated suddenly.

"What the hell is going on?" Allana had barely spoken the words when a loud crack blasted through the tunnels, followed by a powerful shake.

Jadrian pulled her back, catching a last glimpse of his brother as the ceiling collapsed above them, the monastery partially collapsing as the floor gave way. Then the world was black and Jadrian knew nothing of the world around him.

Allana

ALLANA TURNED as the ceiling began to cave in, watching as a pile of timber and stones fell around Jadrian. Swiftly she shifted back to her human form, her face a mask of horror as she began to pull the pile of rubble off Jadrian. With a power few human women would ever know, Allana cleared the largest of the stones and saw Jadrian's face, dirt-covered and battered. He had sustained a crushing blow to the back of his skull, a life-threatening injury that left his scalp torn and a tiny portion of his brain exposed.

Allana sat back, a scream rising in her throat as she inspected the injury. This was surely going to kill him. Throwing more rubble away she saw a sliver of wood had entered his abdomen, just in the right spot to pierce his stomach. Both his arms were broken, as was his right leg. This might be more than even shifter blood could sort. She looked down at him, her face steely.

"You are not going to die, Jadrian, not today."

Allana cleared the rest of the rubble, wishing for a moment she were a vampire, a magical with the power to heal all wounds, but knew that she had to hope her blood, her very old blood, would heal him.

Without anyone else around to give their consent or to debate the merits of what she was about to do, Allana made a decision. She couldn't hear anything from the other side of the rubble blocking their way out of the tunnel, there wasn't anyone to tell her no, that it was a bad idea, so she did the only thing she knew to do.

Shifting to the form of a much smaller house cat, Allana pounced on Jadrian's barely moving chest. His pulse was almost too faint to find, his body already starting to shut down, but Allana found it in his neck, brushing her head against the spot to mark it. With a soft purr she bit deeply into the spot, licking at the blood that began to slowly ooze from the wound. She wasn't doing it to drink his blood, she was doing it to mix her saliva with the blood.

The wound healed quickly, too quickly, and Allana's cat head turned up to his. It didn't work that quickly; it should take days for him to heal. She jumped from his chest and shifted again, sitting beside him as she waited, his hand wrapped in hers, wondering what was going on. She still heard no sounds from outside their tunnel and feared the others might be dead.

Her clan had certainly taken some losses, she could sense the lack of their presence, but not of the other clans. She watched the handsome man in the darkness, considering why she'd changed him. He was an Alexander, of course, but he wasn't a shifter. She'd felt something, something primal and deep, since she'd met him, but he wasn't her mate. Why had she saved him then? Why had she given him this precious gift?

The sudden healing of his head wound distracted her, the skull bone knitting back together and the skin healing before her eyes. She'd pulled the large splinter of wood out of his stomach, noting it was around a foot long, and reset his broken bones, now those injuries were healing too. He still wasn't breathing well, though, and Allana leaned to his chest, pressing her ear to the area where his heart was. She could hear it going from a slow, unsteady beat to a steadier, even sound.

It shouldn't be happening this quickly, she knew, but what she knew and what she saw were totally different things. She turned him over, now that his bones were healed, and looked at his back, pulling his shirt up to look for marks deep enough to leave a scar. Even in the darkness she could see four rows of healed punctures on his back, and knew the marks were from her nails. She'd turned him already and hadn't even known it!

She'd always known it was a possibility to turn humans but she'd never done it by accident before. Allana realized it had saved his life and turned him back over, his body needing rest. She moved until his head rested in her lap, her fingers stroking the side that had not been injured. Whether she had intended it or not, whether she had wanted it or not, this man was now her responsibility, Alexander or not. She'd turned him, she was tied to him forever now. She would care for him as she would her own.

* * *

Jadrian

JADRIAN BECAME aware of the darkness surrounding him, that he was stretched out on the ground, and his head was resting on something soft and warm. Something was stroking his hair and noises pierced the darkness; shouts and the sound scraping filled the air.

"Shh, it is alright Jadrian, our people are working to rescue us." Allana's voice came in the darkness, soothing his nerves. He settled back onto her lap and took a deep breath.

He was trying to remember what happened but all he remembered was the battle, his brother's face as something obscured his vision and he pulled Allana away.

"What…" Jadrian had to pause to clear his throat, something was wrong with him, he could feel it. Something was different. "What happened?"

"The ceiling came down on us. You were injured, gravely injured. Here." She paused to touch his head where the injury had now completely healed. "There, over your stomach, you should feel a scar. Both your arms and your leg, there." She pointed to the place and knew he could see in the darkness when he followed her finger.

"Was? Where? What?" He sat up, exhausted and feeling out of sorts.

"I was going to turn you, make you a shifter to heal you." She turned away, unable to finish. She had turned him by accident before any of this had even occurred.

"Well if you didn't heal me, who did?" He looked around, still not realizing that he could see in the darkness.

"Nobody. You healed yourself." She walked away from him, hoping he would catch her drift.

"Wait, the…" Jadrian stopped himself, not wanting to admit to anyone he had been using vampire blood. "I'm confused."

"You're a shifter, Jadrian! You were already changing, before the injury!" She flung the words out loudly, turning back to him. "Why else do you think you can see me? You feel strange right? Like your head is buzzing, your limbs and stomach feel cold, right? That's from the healing. You started changing at least twenty-four hours ago!"

Jadrian watched her, uncomprehending, as she looked down at the floor before bringing her head back up. He wasn't a shifter, what was she on about?

"Look, Allana—"

"I did it the other day, in bed, by accident! I didn't realize but it doesn't matter now. It saved you! I don't think turning you at this point would have done any good but you were already a shifter before I bit you again." Her words trailed off, her gaze faltering before coming back up to his.

Jadrian began to laugh, his confusion disappearing. The one thing he had always wanted but had never dared ask for! And she'd given it to him by accident without either of them knowing it! He had to bend over, bracing his hands on his knees as he laughed, brushing tears from his eyes.

"Fuck me! By accident!" He howled with laughter until they both heard the people working outside of their tunnel start to shout.

"What's going on in there? Jadrian! Answer me!" Cade's voice sounded muffled through the stones, wood, and dirt between them but he didn't sound far away.

"I'm fine, Cade! Hurry up, will you?" Jadrian was elated to just be alive. He felt the scar on his stomach and knew from the way his head felt that something had happened there as well. He didn't hurt but he felt overwhelmingly strange, as though he were in someone else's body. He was also aware of Allana behind him.

He turned, was about to speak her name, when a new cry came from the other side.

"Jacob? Where the hell have you been?" came Cade's voice.

Jadrian couldn't hear Jacob's answer until he yelled to move back, and Jadrian went to stand with Allana at the back end of the tunnel. A short while later a fist appeared and a beam of light punched through with it. Then another and another until the rubble slid to the side, clearing a path that he and Allana quickly ran through.

Jadrian immediately embraced his brother, and knew something was totally different. Jacob wasn't the same. He looked at his brother and saw he was pale, but little else had changed. He didn't look happy with the world but a lot was going on. Then Cade pulled him into another back slapping hug and they were being ushered up to the surface. Jadrian saw the wives of his brothers and Annie came running at him but she skittered away, backing up with a growl.

"Annie, what's wrong with you?" Damesha came to her dog, trying to soothe the hackles that had raised on the dog's back. The dog was still growling and Jadrian's heart broke as he moved away from her. When the dog barked, Jadrian jumped, or thought he had. When everyone gasped he realized something more had happened.

Looking down Jadrian saw what he was certain were duck feet. The golden orange color was unmistakable and trying to speak only produced a quack. Jadrian ignored the gasps as everybody in the room watched him begin to run in circles squawking his unhappiness to them all!

"Allana, do you care to explain this?" Cade walked up to the other Alpha and looked at her quizzically.

"It is hard to explain but your brother is alive. Without me he wouldn't be. That is all I can tell you for the moment." Allana left him to chase after Jadrian, trying to get him to calm him down.

It was only Damesha that noticed that Annie was still growling but that the growling wasn't directed at Jadrian or the fact that he had become a shifter. No, Annie was staring straight at Jacob, and the low growl she emitted didn't stop until he shifted out of Annie's view. It seemed Jadrian wasn't the only Alexander brother with some explaining to do.

9

Jacob

Jacob noticed Annie growling at him and though he didn't know it, his heart broke knowing that the dog was mistrustful of him. Annie was special, a rather loving dog that melted everyone that came into contact with her. He knew it was his transformation into a vampire that the dog didn't like. She knew him but she knew something wasn't right about him.

He wanted to blend into the crowd and disappear, but knew this had to happen. He'd been away and now, with his clothes and phone returned, he knew he'd been missed. He'd sensed the panic as he left the room he shared with Sabrina, sensed the turmoil going on beneath his feet, and he'd raced to the basement, then below to the tunnels. He'd pushed through the gathered people until he'd been at the wall of rubble and cleared it.

Now that he was found he was forgotten, especially when Jadrian, rather amazingly, turned into a white duck and waddled around the floor quacking his head off. Jacob saw a red-headed woman catch him up and sit trying to soothe him in a rather motherly fashion. A smile played over his lips, obviously he had missed quite a bit.

"Brother, want to tell me why Annie is growling at you?" Cade's voice came with a vice-like clamp on his shoulder.

Jacob turned, a grim look on his face. "Sabrina's coming, can we go somewhere more private?"

Sudden comprehension dawned on Cade's face. "Ah, she's behind this then."

Cade went quiet, studying Jacob more closely as they waited for the vampire to enter the hall they'd made their way to. Another quiet wave of laughter and Jadrian's exasperated voice screaming something about "fuck a duck", let them know he had shifted back to his human form. Both men had a quiet smile on their faces as they listened.

"I guess we're a proper shifter clan now. Did you see

that orange fire in his eyes when you opened the tunnel?" Cade said as he looked at Jacob quizzically. "Yes, a proper shifter family. Are we not?"

Jacob could tell Cade knew from his carefully chosen words. He gave a wobbly nod of his head and was almost weak with relief when Sabrina finally showed up. The appearance of the woman in deep black with the odd stripe of neon pink down her sides, made Jacob's knees wobble. This was his soulmate, the woman his soul had chosen as his forever partner. For vampires, eternity was a long damned time. But first they both had to survive the rage Cade was no doubt about to unleash.

Jacob followed, knowing he had to keep Cade calm and cool. This was huge but not the end of the world. In fact, it was supposed to be the opposite, this was supposed to be the way they saved the world. He was also starting to feel a bit of pique, he was the king of the magical world, even if they didn't know it yet. Why was he following along behind his brother so docilely?

Sure, he'd spent every bit of his thirty-plus years doing as his brother told him but that was all changed now. His pique turned to annoyance as his brother took him to a private office. Jacob continued to follow but he could feel his face was stony by the time he took a seat in the room. He looked up at his brother, defiance etched in every line of his face.

"Who is responsible for this…" Cade paused, waving his hand at Jacob. "Abomination?"

Cade's gaze was as cold as steel on a winter morning in Antarctica. No, this wasn't going to be easy. Jacob inhaled deeply, forming a collection of words that he hoped would not inflame his brother.

"I'm the Alpha now. Of all. Who's fault is that? You could blame our parents, shifters from generations ago, you could blame the Mungons. Or Sabrina. She did only what needed doing."

Oh, those had not been the right words. Cade's face twisted into an angry grimace at Jacob's first sentence.

"Alpha? Of all? I'm the Alpha, I lead the clan." His voice shook with his anger and Jacob could see Cade was barely controlling his urge to pound his fist on the desk.

"Look, Cade, you're a wonderful leader, and you'll remain the leader of our clan, I don't plan to change that, but you're not the king, no matter how you might fit the station. I am."

"I don't see how." Cade, not generally a scoffer, gasped out his disbelief, his face twisting further as he stood, flinging his chair against the wall with the back of his legs. "You are a great helper, Jacob, I can count on you. What makes you think, even as a vampire, that you could take that position? I simply cannot believe you have the gall. After all of these years of hiding in the shadows, what do you think you will gain from all of this?"

"I had hoped I would gain your support, brother. Your help. This is what I get?" Jacob was furious now, his blood boiling.

"I tell you now, brother, I cannot support this. I'm not sure you can even remain a member of our clan, no matter what "decisions" you have made."

Jacob's eyes twitched as his brother made air quotes as he said the word decision. The tips of Cade's hair caught on fire, burning out so quickly that Cade only noticed a sensation that made him brush at his hair.

With now round eyes Jacob tried to hold back a laugh. "You doubt me, brother?"

"I've never seen anything in the way you shift to suggest you would make a great king. Black crows, black mice, sure, you tend to go for black animals, but you don't even have a violent shifter animal, they're creatures that live in the shadows or on carrion."

"You have never seen my back have you, Cade? My shifter animal's mark on my skin. The one animal that rules us all. You've never seen mine have you?" Jacob's words were quietly spoken, a threat there if Cade had only listened.

Cade had never heard that tone from his brother and couldn't possibly understand it now. The menace there, or the warning. Sabrina had sat quietly through the whole exchange but now she cast her eyes to Jacob, her own warning in her gaze.

"This is your brother! Do not make him an enemy!"

Jacob looked back, reassuring her with his own gaze that he would do his best.

"This must be done, be patient, please."

Sabrina lowered her cold blue eyes, acquiescing to her king. But the quirky tilt of her head let him know it was only because they were in public. Jacob's lips wanted to twist into a grin at her but he held it back.

With sure fingers, Jacob plucked at his clothes, pulling his shirt away before turning around.

"What are you doing? It doesn't matter what your spirit animal is…" But Cade's words trailed off, his gaze glued to the dragon stretched out across Jacob's broad shoulders.

The dragon, asleep in the marking that looked like a tattoo but was something more, opened an eye and a stream of smoke to plume from its right nostril. Cade's eyes went round. The animal was black with dark crimson markings, a three-pointed tail, and golden eyes.

"You…well." Cade sat down, his legs going numb. He stared into nothing, stunned. "That doesn't mean anything, it's nothing more than a myth."

"You learn I am a dragon shifter and yet you still dismiss it? As a myth? I knew you loved your position in life, Cade, but this is getting ridiculous!"

"You aren't suited to the position, Jacob!" This time Cade did lose his patience and his fist smashed down on the oak desk with a loud bang. "I love you, brother, but no, this is too much to ask. Did you have any idea of what you were taking on when you made this decision to be turned into a vampire? I have heard some stupid things from Kane and Jadrian but I didn't expect this nonsense from you. You've ruined your life over a myth?"

Cade's face held defeat but defeat at Jacob's choices. He still didn't believe him, Jacob could sense that much.

"Brother, do not destroy our relationship over your own needs, your own selfish desire to be the Alpha." Jacob's words were quiet again, threatening, and this time, Cade heard it.

Dark brown eyes met dark brown eyes across the desk and Jacob stood, his back to the door once more. "Don't say something you cannot take back."

"But why did you decide this, Jacob? Why?" Cade's tone was pleading, he wanted to understand.

Jacob blanched, his gaze going to Sabrina. Jacob's hesitation lasted long enough to let Cade know he hadn't made this decision.

"She took you?" Cade was standing once more, a face full of rage twisted in Sabrina's direction.

"Leave it, what's done is done." Cade began to move

around the desk as Jacob spoke but Jacob held a hand out to him.

Cade's face smashed against an invisible wall, his hands coming up too as he met the wall. "What have you done?"

"You are not to touch her!" Jacob's voice was still quiet but now it held its own threat. Something Cade had never heard from his gentle brother before.

"You may not like this brother, but you have to get over it. What's done is done. Now, can we carry on with our day? I'm sure we need to announce this somehow." Jacob sounded bored now but he knew this wasn't over. Cade wasn't the kind to just let ultimate power slip away. He was too much of a control freak.

The problem wasn't that Cade wanted all of the power, he just didn't think anyone else was capable of wielding it. It was time, now, for him to learn he wasn't alone, that he could rely on others. Whether he liked it or not.

"Jacob, let me out of this!"

"I'm sorry, but no. Not until you chill, Cade. We have some serious shit to sort out and you're being a baby. Now, will you chill or not?" Jacob sat back in his chair, kicking his heels up on the desk nonchalantly as he winked over at Sabrina.

"Jacob!" Cade started to bang against the invisible wall, his hair waving around his head as he shouted.

The problem was Jacob had stolen his voice with a twist of his own fingers and Cade's tirade, though spirited, was now silent. He turned to face Jacob and went to crawl over his desk to get at his brother. With a zip of his finger a new wall went up, and Cade ended up on his ass on the floor.

"Cade, I'm not going to hurt you. I'm not going to let this go to my head, and I'm certainly not going to get us all killed." He shrugged back into his shirt and looked at his brother. "We can get on with what needs doing or we can sit in here until you calm down. Which shall it be?"

Cade looked as though he would like to kill his brother as he crawled back to his feet, and leaned over the desk.

"Do you want more proof? Shall I blast you with energy? Shall I tear down this building? Because if that's what it'll take, I'll give it to you. But I'll never do something to you that will hurt you."

Inspiration struck Jacob at that point. So far he had learned that he just had to think of something, conceive of it, and do something such as snapping his fingers to create the effect. With a gentle smile, Jacob waved his hands down his body, turning himself into an orange light that didn't burn, it was just a glow of orange that shone white in the center, where his soul lived.

With nothing more than a thought, Jacob moved towards his brother. Cade shifted into a wolf, large and as black as Jacob's dragon, and growled at the gleaming being headed for him. Jacob kept moving, engulfing his brother with his light, forcing his love out into the energy, all of the love he felt for his brother encapsulated in the light source. The wolf in the room, still trapped behind invisible walls, settled, his hackles laying down as his legs dropped, and the animal, surrounded by the loving light of his brother, fell into a blissful state where he knew nothing but fraternal love.

"Jacob," Sabrina called to him and the light swirled, coming over to touch her as it expanded, filling the room.

Jacob let her feel his love as well, the moment almost too much for him. With no physical shape he couldn't touch her but his light embraced her too. He loved them both and now they both knew just how much.

With a sound like a sigh, Jacob released them. The light traveled back to the chair he had been in, and Jacob's form took shape once more. He was exhausted but knew the moment would pass. Looking at his brother he saw that Cade had gone back to his human shape, his face stunned. Jacob waved his hand and Cade's voice was given back to him as the walls came down with a tinkling sound of breaking glass.

"Alright, Jacob. We can discuss it all some other time. But yeah, I kind of get it now. We'll see how it goes, shall we?" His shattered eyes, still stunned, gazed at his brothers, so like his own.

"We can do that. I just needed you to accept me, Cade. We can win this coming battle if we stick together. Only together."

"You, well, yes, Jacob. You're our king. That much is obvious now. Let's go."

"Go where?" Jacob asked, confused at his brother's sudden shift to standing and heading out of the room.

"You'll see." An odd smile played around Cade's lips but Jacob trusted his brother, trusted him more than any other man on the planet.

"Alright." Jacob stood, taking Sabrina's hand as she came beside him. "Lead on."

Jacob assumed they were heading for another room and slowed as they came near a private office, but Cade shook his head at his brother and made a gesture for him to keep following. Sabrina walked at Jacob's side with her hand still in his. Her eyes told him to remain calm, all was well. Jacob wasn't so sure. His family was in chaos, there were guards everywhere, and the Mungons had attacked them before they could get the non-fighting magicals out. He thought they were sitting ducks. That reminded him of Jadrian's predicament and he felt his lips twitch for a moment.

Cade stopped in front of a pair of huge doors well over twelve feet tall. Jacob hadn't noticed them before but now he wondered how he could have missed them. Made of solid oak, they looked heavy, but Cade parted them without a problem. Jacob looked at Sabrina, not sure why Cade had brought him here.

"Enter, my liege." Cade bowed, his head going down as he knelt on the cold stone floor.

"What are you doing? Stop that!" But, Cade wouldn't stand, he only gestured into the room.

A sudden wind blew through the monastery and a bell tolled somewhere. Jacob looked around, his confusion deepening. What was going on?

He walked into the chamber, dusty with all of the furniture covered in white cloths. Jacob and Sabrina entered, going ahead to remove the cloth from one piece in particular. Solid silver, the throne was encrusted with jewels and covered with velvet anywhere his skin might touch. Whoa. It was true then.

People began to stream into the room, a buzzing sound accompanying them as they all wondered aloud what was happening. Some knew, others had no idea. As the older magicals streamed in, they came to Jacob where he stood at the throne and knelt. The noise died down as the younger ones caught on and Jacob looked out over a sea of bowed heads.

A new murmur came as the current leaders of the magical world walked through the crowd, striding straight towards Jacob before they too, astonishingly to all present, knelt before him.

"Welcome, your majesty. We greet you with friendship." They stayed on the ground and Jacob looked around uneasily, not used to being in the spotlight.

"Everybody stand up, please. Can somebody help me here?" The couple came to him and guided him to his new throne.

"As the vampire shifter, Jacob, you have joined the two most powerful groups in the magical world. You are now the king of the magicals. Please, take your proper seat."

Jacob sat, looking out at the room with discomfort.

It really was true.

The people looked at him expectantly, as though he were about to impart some universal truth to them that would end all strife. He had nothing in mind, nothing like that anyway. Only a few words of hi, how are you, I'm your king now.

"Listen, folks, I'm new to this so forgive me for not being all "thee and thou" will you? We're facing a great danger here, as you're all aware, my family more than others at the moment. We nearly lost our beloved brother tonight to an infestation of rats. Rats that cannot live. We must take them, destroy them, and ensure peace for all of the magical world. Send out word to all that wish to join the right and good. Come to the sanctuary, join us in our fight!"

Jacob looked out as he spoke, a roar starting to fill the room. They were listening, they'd all accepted him as their leader! Things were changing, where there had been willingness but uncertainty there was now a fierce determination, a positive outlook to the end of this war. Where there had been faces filled with uncertainty and fear there were now faces with hope and righteous certainty that they could win the coming battle. For they were at war and Jacob knew it. He didn't want to fail, was terrified of failing, but his head was full of knowledge and he knew that new skills lurked beneath the surface he just had to figure them out, learn which twitches produced them.

He nodded at Sabrina, Allana and Cade, and they came to him.

"We have plans to make. Cade, I know this is a bit of a shock, that what Sabrina did broke more than a few customs, but we're past that now. What's happened has happened, being angry, starting a war isn't going to change that. We already face a fight that's going to take everything we have to survive. We have a battle to win and bickering over it isn't going to change the fact that I'm now a shifter and a vampire. It's time for battle. Work with me, please?"

"Of course, Jacob. What's done is done now, and

perhaps Sabrina was right. It's time for drastic measures. Obviously the Mungons are bent on destruction. And from what I've now seen, I know that you're the man for the job."

Jacob could see Cade's face was hard but accepting. He had kept to his word, whether he liked it or not.

10

Jacob

"No, death is the only option for this vermin!" Jacob clapped his hand down on the table and glared at the alien couple next to him. He would not have recognized himself a month ago, strong, charismatic, and decisive. Some were even whispering that he was a hard man, ruthless, but necessarily so. "I'm not going to allow them to come back a year from now and start this all over again! Have you paid attention to what has been happening in the world? If we don't annihilate the whole bunch of them, they'll come back. Sure, there might be another faction that forms later but we'll deal with that then. For now, we deal with the Mungons. All of them!"

"As you wish, majesty." The alien couple moved as

one, making a placating gesture. "You are right of course. We have been too diplomatic I suppose. As the king it is your place to judge. If you find them lacking they will be dealt with."

The couple had come to him to ask him to try diplomacy once more. Jacob had left the current government intact but had retained the final say. He wanted to know the will of his people, and he knew it now. It was death for all adult Mungons.

"Is there a world we could send them to, perhaps?" Jacob asked, a moment of weakness making him ask the question.

"Not one that they could not eventually escape. It might take them hundreds of years but they would make their way back to our world." The couple, still so pale it made Jacob squint, touched their fingertips together, hands tapping together, as the creatures thought. "No, you are right, Jacob. There is nowhere we could send these beings without them causing death where they go, and eventually coming back to us."

So far, no children had been found in the enclaves, mainly because, as they knew now from questioning prisoners, the Mungons didn't have children, they made them. Children were vulnerable, weak, and could go either way when it came to personality so the Mungons turned adults instead, refusing for the most part to reproduce naturally. The knowledge saved Jacob's heart and brain some distress but still, people were dying, and it didn't sit easily on his shoulders. He had a moment of hope when he'd asked about another planet but now he knew he had to continue making the hard decisions that burdened him greatly.

A month had passed and the Mungons were being flushed from their enclaves, and Jacob hated all of the death, he hated the monster he considered himself to be now, but he was a leader. He had to protect his people and the unsuspecting mortal world that had no idea of the battle raging to save them. If it required mountains of death, so be it. He sighed as the room emptied, and Sabrina came to him, her hand joining his as she perched on the arm of the chair.

"It's not easy, I know, but you're doing well, Jacob. Throughout the world the Mungons are being hunted down, at the will of the people, not just at your direction. Don't shoulder all the guilt for what we all do, what's been done." Her words soothed him but they didn't take away the burden of being a death-dealer.

"I'll be fine. How are you today?" He had softened to her over the last few weeks, his need for her burning hotly still, but his emotions became entangled with hers and they faced the knowledge they were mated with acceptance. He knew his soul had chosen her but there was still something in him that was cold towards her, an anger that he thought would never leave him. Sighing once more, he waited for her answer.

"I'm fine, as usual. I'd like to get you into bed again, but I know you're busy." She soothed a hand down his face, leaning into his body. A vampire needing comfort, Jacob almost snorted, but held it back as he brushed a hand over hers.

"It's been a long month. I've had to cloak our activities from the non-magicals, answer calls from all over the world and try to ensure we're not all murdered in our sleep. There's been little time. I'm sorry." He looked up at her with apology, his heart melting just a little as he looked at her.

She filled his head all the time and Jacob didn't know if that was their connection or the fact that his soul yearned for her. They were never far apart, but they'd had little time for sex or love. She was so innocent looking, and knowing that what she'd done had been done for a reason made it better but still, there was a part of him that wanted to throttle her still. Or fuck her into the middle of next week.

"Perhaps later? I will steal away for an hour, shall I?" He kissed her, his lips brushing hers and she gasped in surprise at the sudden peace offering he gave her.

"Of course." She leaned into his lips once more, brushing a hand over his chest. His heart thumped and his hands went to her hip, pulling her towards him.

"Or now?" He looked up into her eyes, smiling a teasing smile.

She smiled back and was about to give a sultry response when a throat cleared behind them.

"Uh, sorry, Jacob. I'm back from the raid in Texas," Cade said, bashful.

"Later," Jacob promised as she stood and looked at Cade. He hadn't made her officially his consort but she stayed at his side just the same.

"I need to speak with Adrian, I'll be in our chamber later."

"Alright. I'll see you later, then."

Sabrina

SABRINA MOVED THROUGH THE HALLS, heading for her room. She met Adrian there and they sat in a pair of chairs. Sabrina sighed and looked at the man across from her. Her consort for hundreds of years, now her best friend and always would be, even if their romantic relationship was all but dead.

"I think he's coming around." She finally spoke, hope in her voice. A strong, stony woman in public, but with Adrian she could reveal the vulnerability she had only shown otherwise to Jacob during his transformation.

"Shall I unpack the bags then?" Adrian's voice sounded bored but Sabrina knew better.

He was just as curious to see what would happen next as she was. He just didn't have the added burden of loving the man she knew hated her. She could feel the burning ember of his hatred deep inside, though he tried to hide it from her. The fire was burning out over time. As her love grew, the fire dimmed.

"At least he really was the dragon shifter. That's a blessing." Adrian gave voice to a thought he'd had doubts about. "I'm glad you didn't listen to me when I doubted your plan."

"As am I. I'd heard rumors but didn't know for sure until that night in the alley. I saw him and he was magnificent!" Her voice and eyes burned with a fascination and admiration Adrian had never seen from her before. He knew she was remembering the night she'd seen him in the alley, when he'd flown into the air, becoming the most magnificent dragon she'd ever seen.

"Ah, you're in love!" Adrian's tone changed to teasing and his mouth quirked into a devilish smile. "My little princess, in love again!"

There was no rancor in his voice, no jealousy, just affection.

Sabrina giggled and covered her mouth, her eyes going round. "Holy hell, I just giggled!"

"Well, my dear, even Scarlett O'Hara let out the occasional giggle." They'd been to the premier of the movie starring said heroine in Atlanta on the day of its release and it had been a favorite ever since.

"You're quite right, she did!" Sabrina's voice, tinged with a slight accent but not that most people would notice, was broken up with giggling again.

"So he is coming tonight?" Adrian's left eyebrow quirked, wondering if he could join them. That Jacob was a rather handsome fellow.

"Yes, but you can't come. I think I'd like him on my own for tonight." Her own eyebrow quirked as she stuck her tongue out at him.

"Like that is it? You are in love!" Adrian gave her a catty grin but then took her hand. "I think, my darling, that you have to give him time. I've watched the Alexanders and they're a broody lot. Every single one of them, but they love passionately, deeply, and fiercely. Give Jacob time, he will come around."

"Oh, stop patting my hand!" Sabrina stood up, feeling foolish as tears sprang to her eyes. "This is so silly! But I can't help it. He's just so…amazing!"

"Right now he needs someone to lean on, pet. Give him that, give him what he needs. He's making decisions that will haunt him for the rest of his life. He has to make those decisions but they aren't easy ones to make. What he's doing is right in the eyes of all of us in the magical world, he's destroying those that would destroy us, but that is a hard choice to make."

"I know. I do. I can only try." Sabrina had waited over the weeks, waited for him to thaw, to come to her for sex, for any sign that he wasn't going to hate her forever. She'd stood at his side, waited for him to offer some affection, but he'd been too busy. Now he was coming and her stomach knotted.

As a vampire, she didn't need to go through the preparations human women had to make, but she needed to dress, needed to set the ambiance, needed to make sure he found her desirable.

She'd given Jacob a new life, given the world hope, and had won his coldness for her efforts. She understood, but he'd shown a sign of thawing and now she was going to take it and run with it.

"Yes, unpack the bags, I need something else to wear. And the candlesticks we brought, I want those out and lit. Oh, there is so much to do, don't just sit there, move Adrian!"

They both laughed as she prodded him out of his chair, running around the room. It might be alright for her after all.

Jacob

"Look, I've done nothing but pace around offices, stare at maps, make plans, and sit on that fucking throne for a month now. You're all going to give me an hour to take a shower, sit down with a glass of wine and spend a few minutes on my own, do you understand? Do you?" Jacob looked around the room angrily, thumping his hand on the arm as someone came to him, asking about wall hangings. "I don't give two fucks if there are velvet Elvis paintings on the fucking walls or Renoir, I just don't give a fuck. Decide for yourselves, it's your room, I just work here!"

Jacob stalked off and heard Cade chuckling behind him. He turned back to his brother, giving him the finger before stalking off. Cade laughed louder and Jacob couldn't help but grin. Cade was cool with it all now and found the moments when Jacob lost his cool, not a frequent occurrence, amusing. Yeah, alright, perhaps he'd overdone it a little. But he'd not been able to get Sabrina out his mind since she'd left him. He needed to see her, taste her, be inside of her.

He needed her.

Stalking to their chamber, a room he'd rarely visited over the last few weeks, Jacob pushed at the door and strode into the dimly lit room. She'd lit candles on a table, the long tapers making the room glow. A bottle of wine, two empty glasses and a plate of cheese and olives sat on the table.

She'd been waiting for him then.

Closing the door, he finally saw she was in bed, asleep. He knew vampires could sleep, he'd done it himself, but they didn't need it as much as humans did. They could do it at will, as well. She must have decided to sleep the hours away until he came.

Undressing, he pulled the covers back, and slid between into the luxurious cotton sheets. He was glad she preferred the material over the satin some women thought was romantic. He hated the stuff, but cotton soothed him better than anything else.

He absorbed the feeling for a moment, the first time he'd really been comfortable in weeks. He could lie here forever, he thought, but soon her scent drifted to him and he turned his head to her. Her eyes were open, calmly staring at him.

"Hi," he said, running a finger down her cheek.

"Hi," she said, settling into her pillow deeper. "All finished?"

"I don't think I'll ever be finished, but yeah, I told them to fuck off for an hour." He gave a small laugh and she smiled at him.

"You'll have to do that more often. It is good for them to know you have boundaries and needs. You're not a machine, you know?" She shifted, her smooth leg coming to slide up his thigh before going over his waist. She was naked beneath the mountain of covers.

Jacob ran a hand up her silky skin, stopping when his hand found the roundness of her bottom. He heard her sigh and filed the sound away to memory. He loved that sound from her. His hand went higher, pulling her closer as he did so.

"I'll try to remember that." He wanted to kiss her but something made him hold back, a need to explore her further. Shifting, he pulled her on top of him. "Let me look at you."

She looked down at him, her hair around her shoulders and pooling at her bottom. Her skin, naturally pale, was almost translucent since she'd become a vampire. He loved the way her hips flared out, the way her waist tucked in, and wished he was a painter. He would paint her just like this.

A finger brushed down from her ribs, testing the silkiness of her skin. She shivered and he looked up into her face to see her giggling.

"That tickled."

"Ah, and is tickling bad?" A very playful tone had found its way to his voice.

"Tickling is right next to all of the other things that will get you burned at the stake."

"So no tickling?" His fingers brushed at her ribs and she moved, hovering somewhere around the ceiling.

"No tickling." She gave a wiggle of her eyebrows and slowly came down from the ceiling.

"Oh, that could be useful. What else can we do?" He wanted to know but later, he realized as she settled into his arms, her lips pressing to his.

Jacob closed his eyes as he kissed her, a peaceful feeling settling over his head as his body stirred to life. A throbbing had started in his groin, a pleasant feeling that made him want to twist into her, but she wasn't positioned for it.

"Open your eyes, Jacob." She'd stopped kissing him and spoke as she tasted his lips with her tongue. Her hands had gone around his waist and he opened his eyes to see they were floating off of the bed. His eyes went round and he realized he wasn't going to fall.

"We aren't going to fall, it's alright. Just move." Her lips brushed his as she spoke and he focused on them.

He was amazed at this new ability, but he was more concerned about tasting her again. She still tasted of peaches and he loved it. Dipping his tongue into her mouth he stroked her tongue with his, teasing it to twine with his.

He held her to him, her body on top of his but weightless. His hands went to her bottom, kneading the round globes as she moaned into his mouth. He'd missed her touch, he realized. She began to stroke his back, her nails gliding softly down his skin as she moved to the front and found his nipples. She teased him, scraping a nail gently over one of his nipples. His inhaled breath, sudden and surprised, let her know he liked it.

"Not afraid of a little pain, then. Good." He saw she had a rather kittenish look on her face, a look that beguiled him with its sensuality.

"Not at all, princess. Not at all."

Sabrina scraped the nipple harder, stopping to squeeze it as he hissed once more. Jacob felt the touch go all the way to his dick and wanted more from her. She gave it to him by pinching the tight skin between her fingers before flicking her tongue over it.

"Oh, fuck me." He groaned the words as she sucked at the silky skin, her tongue darting over it easily.

"I plan to," she whispered, before going back to his nipple, her hand going down to stroke his abdomen and teasing him as each circling stroke went lower.

He was panting in the air as her teasing attentions went on, his body craving more.

"Fuck, I want to taste you!" He groaned as his mouth sucked at her finger, needing something more, her taste to fill his mouth with. He felt her moving away and opened his eyes to see her body turning, her feet now where her head had been. With a quirked eyebrow he took her meaning, his mouth watering as he pulled her closer, higher.

As her mouth sank down onto him, Jacob moaned, his

ass tensing to press him deeper into her hot depths. But he didn't allow himself to be lost in her until he found her center with his own mouth, his tongue delving between the folds to find the heart of her pleasure. His lips sucked at the tiny bud, making her moan, and his fingers sank into her depths. The two fingers sank as deep as he could press them and her walls tightened around him slickly.

Jacob felt a shiver go down his spine as he tasted her, felt her, and inhaled her scent. She had pulled away as his mouth found her but she started her exploration of him once more, her tentative strokes now a fierce hunger to have him in her mouth. She went down on him, letting him deeply into her throat, and Jacob felt the walls of the tiny passage pressing around his hard length.

The crown of his cock throbbed as he flexed his hips into her, her nails digging into his hips as she held onto him. His head was full of her, the way she felt, tasted, smelled, the way she touched him, and he felt as though he were vibrating, on the edge of exploding. He wanted to be buried balls deep in her pussy, he didn't want to spill in her throat, he wanted to look into her eyes as he fucked her hard and fast.

"Then that's what you'll have, Jacob." She purred to him as she sucked her way up his dick and took him out of her mouth. Turning once more she sank down onto him, her smooth legs wrapping around his back as her opening split for him, taking him smoothly.

"Fuck! More, more Sabrina!" He wanted it all, every bit of her. But he didn't know what else she could give him.

Placing a wrist against his lips she spoke to him. "Drink."

He looked at her uncertainly but did as she instructed. As his fangs came out to pierce her flesh she began to rock on him, moving on his shaft easily, as her red tongue flashed out, licking her bottom lip. He inhaled deeply as he watched her, quickly losing his control as her blood hit his tongue, pleasure exploding in his brain and his dick. He breathed through his nose, his hips thrusting roughly into her, his brain somewhere he couldn't define, as he drank from her.

They moved together as one. The way he stretched her made him gasp as her tight walls pulsed around him and he growled intensely. Sabrina cried out his name as she began to rock harder, faster. Jacob held her hips, fucking into her as she squeezed around his dick, her pulsing walls driving him on. With a deep moan he felt the first brain-blowing blast of his release, his teeth clamping down on her wrist as he followed her over the edge.

But it didn't stop there, it didn't stop at all as she pulled her arm away and settled her hands on his shoulders. Oh no, she somehow began to ride him harder, deeper, and he felt like she was fucking his entire body, not just his dick. Sabrina engulfed him somehow, took all of him, and he could have sworn he was looking down at himself looking up at her.

Jacob felt his control slip and turned with her, found he had managed to put them back on the bed, and that Sabrina was now on her knees. He was still inside of her as he pounded into her from behind, their skin moving together slickly, bodies still joined, and he came again, going even higher than he thought was possible. He heard her beneath him, screaming his name, knowing she was coming as well, but he was her, and she was him, and nothing could tear that apart.

Then the world was black, and he slept, Sabrina curled in his arms, their bodies needing each other even in sleep. He dreamed of her, of a future where she whispered her love to him, and wondered if it could really happen. Could she love him, could he ever love her? Perhaps so, when this was all over.

11

Jadrian

"Good morning, Annie, you precious little puppy, what are you doing today?" Jadrian kissed the loveable dog on the side of her face, her snout coming up to let him know she would accept his kiss but he had better give her a good scratching as well. At least she wasn't teasing him with trails of crackers and little hard plastic pools of water such as the one he had found in his room when he woke up this morning.

Jadrian's hands clenched around Annie's ears where he was scratching and she protested with a quiet yelp and a toss of her head. "They put a fucking kiddy pool in my bedroom while I was asleep, Annie! Bastards!"

She gave him a lick and looked at him as if to say, "fuck 'em, I still love you."

"I love you too, you sweet little thing. Let's get some breakfast." The dog followed him as he clung to the shadows of the hallways, avoiding people and their eyes as he went.

He'd always wanted to be like his brothers but had been afraid of what it might mean. He'd admired their strength, their stamina, the way they could change into anything they wanted—almost. But this wasn't what he'd had in mind. Since that first humiliating shift he'd not made another attempt, and he'd avoided Allana.

Not because he was angry with her but because of the way she'd been holding him while he was still a duck. He'd been totally emasculated and he knew it. A duck shifter, he scoffed to himself as they finally ended up in the dining hall. Just what he'd always wanted to be!

Jadrian spotted Cade and waved. Filling two plates, one for him and one for Annie, Jadrian made his way to the Alpha.

"How's it going?" Jadrian asked as he sat at one of the long benches filling the room. The room was a scene from an ancient castle with rough-hewn tables and benches taking the place of elegant dining tables and chairs. This wasn't meant to be a place of comfort, after all, just feeding.

"Fine, I guess. I haven't seen the ladies yet. How are

you?" Cade looked distracted, Jadrian noted, but filled his mouth with pancakes before answering.

"Still trying to decide what to do with myself. Ducks aren't intimidating, and definitely aren't good for much in battle." He tucked another piece of bacon into his mouth as he finished, handing a piece down to Annie. The dog took it delicately but made it disappear in one bite.

"You'll have to keep trying, Jadrian. You're not limited to one animal, you know? You'll find one you feel most at home in, but you're not locked into one choice." Cade sipped at his coffee, his eyes still on the door. "When you find that one animal, your spirit animal, it will live on your body somewhere, as a tattoo. What's Mary doing here?"

Jadrian looked up to see an almost exact copy of Annie coming into the doorway. Jacqui, Cade's wife, had wanted a dog just like Annie and, as a witch, had managed to make it happen, to her own surprise. And theirs. None of them had known she was a witch when she'd first come to them, not even Jacqui herself.

Cade gave a short whistle that caught the dog's attention and she came trotting over to Cade, a whine escaping her as she scuttled near. Jadrian had never seen the dog act so submissive with her bottom low, tail tucked between her legs, and head down as she came to Cade.

"What's wrong with her?" Jadrian asked and Annie went over to her twin, licking her as both dogs began to whine in unison, their bodies doing an awkward dance of distress.

"Now they're both at it! Where are the girls at?" Jadrian looked around but didn't see Damesha or Jacqui anywhere. A tingle of apprehension went down his spine. Something wasn't right.

Jacob came into the hall, making a beeline for Jadrian and Cade.

"Come with me." The brother, the one that had lived in the shadows for so long, was now giving commands and walking away with certainty that they'd be followed. Cade and Jadrian went without question.

Jacob was the king of the magicals now, his words were law. Everybody had accepted it. He was the only shifter that had survived being transformed into a vampire as well. He was the king of kings.

Jadrian's unease didn't settle down as the dogs followed along, their whines not stopping. He knew that this wasn't going to be pleasant, whatever it was. Jacob hadn't summoned them in such a way ever before. He knew it was to do with the women, that was apparent from the dogs. They rarely left their ladies this long, and with the whining, Jadrian knew something bad had happened.

Fear knotted his stomach, fear of what had

happened, what was about to happen, but he suppressed it. He was an Alexander after all. They didn't do fear, ever.

He just wanted this over, he thought, as he glared at his brothers' backs, feeling a moment of doubt return. What was the good of having a vampire shifter and all of these Alphas floating around if the issue wasn't handled? Why were they now following Jacob to another chamber, dread making all of their hearts pound as these poor animals cried like this? Too much inactivity was making Jadrian restless and the tenseness of the situation made his attitude even worse.

"Right. Two things." Jacob turned as he entered the chamber, Jadrian closing the door. "Allana, Damesha, Sabrina and Jacqui are missing."

Jadrian cringed as he heard Cade roaring beside of him and he turned to his brother to offer a steadying hand. His own stomach dropped out as Jacob said Allana's name. She was gone too. Who had her and why? That was all he wanted to know as he started thinking up ways to kill whatever prick had taken her.

"We also think Allana took them." Jacob's words were spoken quietly and without inflection.

"What?" Jadrian's dark blond eyebrow raised, disbelief making his face twist. "No, that's not possible. Why?"

"We have had some intel. Allana is the Mungons'

leader's daughter." Jacob's face remained impassive, no blame or accusations being made.

Jadrian felt the world fall from under his feet. His initial distrust and the sense that she was up to something had been correct then. So she hadn't actually given a shit about him at all, she'd been using him as a pawn. He wanted to break things, tear walls down with his bare hands, but instead he stared at the floor, taking deep breaths as he wrestled his anger. At least he hadn't fucked her. He'd avoided her since that near tragedy in the tunnel, and now he was glad he had. He hadn't seen this coming at all.

"His daughter? How? They don't breed!" Jadrian had been to all of the meetings about the Mungons and what was happening, he knew the information about the group.

"It seems the psychopath took a bride a couple of centuries ago, they had one daughter. She ran away at eighteen and from what we know, hasn't been back since. She let it be known she hated her father and this could very well be a ploy of hers, but we don't know. Are you two ready to go?"

Jadrian didn't have to be told where they were going or what to expect. If the Mungons had the Alexander women they were going to get them back, come hell or high water. Finally, something to do.

Jadrian's jaw popped as he ground his back teeth

together. The first one he wanted to see was Allana. Not for answers, he knew her reasons now that he knew who her father was. He just wanted to watch her being chained and taken away for her betrayal of him and the magical world.

"Let's roll." Cade's tone was calm, deadly, and cold.

Yeah, Jadrian was pretty certain they were bringing a little death and a whole lot of hell to the Mungons today. He just needed the knots in his stomach to go away.

Jacob

JACOB'S INSIDES were roiling so much he could barely stand it. The woman he'd come to understand was his soulmate was far away and he was certain that Kane and Cade were feeling even worse. He couldn't sense Sabrina and wondered how the shifter had lured her away. She wouldn't have been able to render Sabrina unconscious, she must have lured her somehow.

Jacob didn't know what Allana had planned, but whatever it was, taking the women wasn't cool. She would answer every question he had when he found her, one way or another. She would pay.

Kane soon came through the door, his hair twisting in dozens of directions from his fingers combing through it every five seconds. Jacob felt his anger, his fear and frustration. As their king he felt responsible for what was happening and knew he couldn't fail now, it simply wasn't an option. The wives of his brothers, and indeed their lives, all depended on getting them back.

Standing together the brothers felt some inner instinct working within them, and they moved closer, their hands coming out to lock together in the middle of the circle they formed. With eyes blazing they all focused on the woman they were tied to and let their instincts guide them. An orange light grew in the room, as though a fire were turning into an inferno around them, and with a flash of light the brothers disappeared.

This was their battle now.

12

Jacob

Somewhere in West Virginia

A low static sound broke the night sounds of a mountain deep in the heart of West Virginia coal country. As the sound cracked the night a flash of orange fire briefly lit up the night. Anyone glancing out would dismiss the flash as a trick of their eyes, as the rumored foxfire said to plague the hills, or an odd flash of the millions of fireflies that turned the night into a fairy forest.

As Jacob looked around he stared in awe as tiny greenish yellow lights winked off and on, and for a moment he knew why fairy stories were told. Nights like this, filled with reality but hued with a sense of magic in an age without science. Then his own reality sank in and he dismissed his wonder. Fairies were real after all, not glowing bugs in the darkness. He looked at his brothers and found their eyes on him, waiting for his direction.

Jacob had begun to adjust to his new position but sometimes he still felt a moment of doubt. He had no time for doubt now. His plan was clear.

"We go in hard, fast, shifted. I go in first. No, Cade, before you start, I'll go first. You know that'll be for the best, trust me." Jacob had yet to reveal he wasn't just a vampire shifter but a vampire dragon shifter to his other brothers, only to Cade. He was all but invincible and he knew it, he was going in first.

"I hear you, brother. I don't like it, but I hear you." Cade closed his mouth again and leaned against a scrubby pine tree, one of the many trees dotting the mountainside.

Jacob looked up for a moment, seeing the moonlight. It had taken them longer to get here than he thought, he realized suddenly. It had been morning when they left but now it was night. Or maybe the forest canopy was so thick in these hills that it looked like night all the time. Either way, he had a job to do.

"Alright, Jadrian, I want you to shift. Concentrate on

something—anything that will give you strength and power, you hear me? Go ahead." Jacob knew that Jadrian had been hesitant to shift since that first time and wanted to get this out of the way. If Jadrian shifted into something harmless they needed to sort that now.

Jadrian closed his eyes, his face a mask of concentration and in an instant another creature had taken his place. All of the brothers stared down at the creature shorter than Jadrian's normal stature with awe, impressed at his choice. This was an animal that could fight.

Jacob looked down at the silverback gorilla staring up at him with glowing orange eyes.

"That'll do just fine, well done. The rest of you?" Jacob looked at his brothers expectantly.

Kane shifted into a brown bear, his claws long and capable of flaying flesh from bone. Cade went for the black panther again, his blond streak back above his eyes. Jacob intended to save his for the moment he needed it. No need to try and ramble through the area as a cumbersome dragon.

Leaning on his instincts once more, Jacob led the small group through the woods until he found an abandoned mine shaft. Something was pulling him in that direction, some invisible force that he couldn't explain. His gut told him the few surviving Mungons were down there hiding in the darkness, holding the women as insurance for their lives.

He peered into the darkness, his vampire eyes making it seem almost like daylight once he'd focused. He doubted his instincts for a moment, doubted there was anyone in there. There had to be, though, this is where his instincts, his search for Sabrina through the ether, had led him.

A low growl from behind him and a nudge from Cade's panther head let him know his brothers agreed; this was the place. Jacob knew some of those interrogated had mentioned a place such as this but hadn't believed it. From that intel alone he knew there must be dozens of Mungons down there but he didn't sense any of them. Jacob stepped into the shaft, his brothers stalking behind him.

They followed the shaft and went further down until the cold and damp turned into a steady heat and the air became stuffy. Jacob had no idea how men could work down here, crawling along shafts that went from head height to passages they practically had to crawl through. They walked for a half hour before they heard anything.

The shaft they'd followed, one of many, turned to the right and he edged to the end, seeing the faint flickering in flames on the wall. A man stood there on his own, playing a game on his phone.

On silent feet Jacob moved towards the man, not realizing he had turned into a form of fog until he reached out and punched the man in the head. The man looked up as he felt something brush his face but saw only a mist. He examined it but saw nothing so went back to his game. Jacob changed in a flicker, turning human once more, and punching the man in the head, knocking him out.

Jacob knew the Mungons leader was close. They were down here and stupidly burning something for light. Jacob might have grown up a farm boy in Kansas but even he knew you didn't allow so much as a spark down in a coal mine, the places were notorious for filling up with explosive methane without anyone realizing it. The idiots had placed themselves in danger that went beyond just taking the women.

There was some kind of room that had been dug into the space off to the left, voices came from the area, but that was it. There wasn't even a guard posted, as far as he could see. Too easy, his instincts screamed. Far too easy.

What might not be easy was the mass of Mungons rejects not far below. Jacob could sense them now, their anger, their thirst for blood, but not the blood of their leader. Those shifters still wanted to fight for their leader, to have a chance to prove themselves once more.

Fanatics that would do anything. Jacob shuddered, hoping they wouldn't find their way free.

He looked back at his brothers, tried to urge caution with his eyes, and went into the shaft heading straight for the room he had spotted. Sabrina was close, and he felt his heartbeat pick up the closer he got to her.

Sabrina

SABRINA STARED at the people sitting around a tall rough pine wire spool, obviously something that had been used down in the mine. The men sat on wooden boxes with the words "dynamite" printed on them. How long had it been since those boxes were brought down here? Were they really sitting on dynamite or had the boxes been emptied? Stupid men. Her gaze shifted as the men, six of them, finally turned to the woman sitting at the end, her hands tied behind her back.

Allana, the shifter Alpha with the flaming red hair. Sabrina planned to drain her of blood and life as soon as she was freed from the enchanted chains wrapped around her wrists and waist. Sabrina had known other chains like the ones she'd used on Jacob existed but she didn't realize anyone in America had them. They were an ancient tool, expensive and hard to come by.

They also worked on vampires, though they didn't burn her skin, they simply rendered her muscles too weak to fight. Sabrina felt her fangs slide out of her gums as she watched the women. A man began to speak, a handsome man but for the cruel twist of his lips.

"So the prodigal daughter returns, bearing gifts as well." His hand spread out to indicate Sabrina, Jacqui and Damesha. He looked them over, his sneer somehow growing deeper, his eyes becoming ugly with hateful glee. He had a bargaining tool now. And if the Alexanders didn't want to play ball, well, he would enjoy torturing each woman to death.

Sabrina saw his thoughts and felt her own anger growing. She didn't need the Alexander men to take this piece of shit out. She just needed to somehow break these chains.

"Father, I did as you bid me. I went out and found a new clan decades ago. They adopted me and kept me safe. They learned to trust me, and in time I became their Alpha. I brought you the women of our sworn enemies. I come in peace, please untie me," Allana pleaded pitifully, her eyes round with an innocence Sabrina had never seen before.

She was this monster's daughter and she was truly loyal to him. Holy hell! The news of Allana's parentage somehow didn't shock Sabrina but her duplicity did.

Sabrina had taken little interest in the other woman

but wished she had now. She'd seemed like another arrogant shifter, not worth Sabrina's notice, but now Sabrina saw that was probably what Allana had hoped for. Jadrian must be whipping himself into a frenzy of hatred if he knew that Allana was behind this. If anyone even realized they were missing at all.

She knew that as a shifter, Jacob was probably aware of her absence. The soul mating would not allow them to be separated for long before the consequences would be felt. That meant Cade had to be aware of it too. Jacob's vampirism would protect him partly but Cade didn't have that protection. Would they be able to fight? Sabrina didn't know how quickly being separated from a soulmate would affect a shifter.

Sabrina went back to listening to the group as Allana spoke once more.

"Please, father? How can you doubt me?"

"I haven't seen you in over a century, daughter. Why?"

"You told me to let the world think I hated you! How was I supposed to contact you and make them believe it?" Allana appeared desperate and that made Sabrina start to wonder.

Allana could be afraid the brutal man sitting beside her would kill her, but did that totally explain her desperation? Sabrina watched as the beautiful woman collected herself, her pale skin flushing slightly as she sat back. Sabrina could see Allana was wondering if she had overstepped herself.

"I suppose you're right, daughter. You've brought me the Alexander women. The Alpha of the clan must already be feeling the effects of being so far from his mate. It's just a pity there are only three of them. I'd have liked to take them all out." James waved a hand at one of the other men around the table and looked bored with the whole thing.

Sabrina started to form a plan as she watched the exchange that ended with Allana being freed. She looked over at the other women and caught their eyes. She knew Jacqui was a witch, Damesha a psychic and she used those skills to communicate with the women quietly.

"Can you use your powers to free yourself, Jacqui?" The thought obviously hit its target when Jacqui tensed and looked over at her. A subtle nod of the witch's head let her know Jacqui knew it was her.

"Good, do it quietly, then free Damesha."

Sabrina was certain the men would want them to sit quietly until they came to the rescue but that wasn't her style. She hadn't lived for centuries without learning how to survive dangerous situations.

A few moments later a warm hand nudged hers, and Sabrina resisted the urge to jump. It was just Jacqui letting her know she was free. It was Sabrina's turn to nod her head softly.

"Now, can you free me?" They were all huddled on the floor in a corner of the room, left in the shadows as the Mungons made plans for their dwindling future.

"We're not done yet and now with my daughter and her clan here to help, they'll not be so fast to attack us. If they can even figure out where we are. Even with that clown they have claiming my throne, they're not going to find us here." James spoke with a sneer that Sabrina was hoping to remove from his face, permanently.

That 'clown' was her man, not the joke this cretin was trying to make him out to be. She still wasn't sure what she needed to do but she didn't feel like sitting around waiting for someone to come and save her. Jacqui nudged her hand once more and Sabrina turned to her, wordless, as the other woman's hand clasped hers. Her chains fell away and Sabrina tensed, ready to make her move.

* * *

Jacob

JACOB LISTENED AT THE DOOR, hearing the murmur of people within. He knew Allana was in the room but didn't know the others. He also knew the women were in there but he didn't sense Sabrina. He moved around, trying to hear what was being said. A shout came from the other end of the shaft and Jacob turned, blasting the man with a bright white light that made him disintegrate into a pile of dust.

He heard the startled sounds his shifted brothers made but ignored them as he made a sudden decision, time to end this. He pushed into the door, forcing the warped wood open as his brothers took up a position behind him. Bullets wouldn't hurt him, knives couldn't kill him, he was invincible as he walked into the room. That is, until he saw Sabrina standing tall and proud on the other side of the room. He knew he loved her in that instant, but didn't have the time to ponder over it as they were all in danger.

She stood there, palm pointed at the table, the full brunt of her regal anger focused on a man sneering at the table. His heart stopped for a moment as he took in her beauty, as he felt love making his head spin, when a gun was pointed at Damesha's head, the woman standing behind Sabrina but not covered enough to be out of the way of bullets.

Pushing down the sudden wobbliness of his knees, Jacob strode into the room, his black leather work boots making a hollow thump on the rock floor, and clawed his hands into the shirt of the man sneering at the table and pulled him across the wooden spool.

"You want to be king? You're barely qualified to run a low-budget diner and you want to rule over the entire magical realm? You're a total joke." Throwing him against the wall, Jacob watched the man's head bounce, hoping the landing split his skull.

Jacob's hand shot out for the next one, a scraggly looking little prick with a narrow face and dirty hair. That one went flying as well, the others taking off at a run before Jacob could get to them but coming to a sudden halt when they saw the shifted brothers. They stood stock still with nowhere to run, their eyes huge as they began to plead.

"Look, we'll do what you want, just let us go. We'll even tell you where he hid your parents' bodies! Please, would you not like to give them a proper burial?" The Ratman's eyes peered up at Jacob, his hopes growing.

The room had come to a complete standstill, Jacob in the middle. His eyes shifted to Allana's, and he gave her credit for not cowering. She sat there defiantly, eyes wide as he strode over to her.

"I'm not sure what to do with you yet, but you'll have a chance to speak, to tell us your side. Later."

He'd sensed bodies moving up from the depths of the mine, and knew they had little time. Turning to his brothers, he walked out of the room knowing Sabrina would keep the leaders in the room. She was magnificently furious but cold as she moved behind him, pinning the men to the walls with her eyes alone. She did have a rather stunning gaze.

Taking a deep breath, he moved out into the hallway, the tide of shifters looking like a wave as they jumped over each other to get to the brothers. Even after decades of being trapped below, they were still loyal to the one who'd put them there. He knew what he had to do, though he might not have enough room, even with the taller ceiling in this area.

Shifting into his dragon form, Jacob looked down at the tide of shifters. They moved as one and twitched as one. His was hunched down to fit into the narrow space, but he had room.

With a deep breath into his massive dragon lungs, Jacob breathed out, the dragon brain taking over the human as fire blazed from his mouth. He felt the heat but it didn't burn him and it poured out his throat like napalm, coating the moving mass aimed at him and his brothers. They all came to a halt as the fire poured over them, the force of the blast stopping them in their tracks just as much as being covered in liquid fire did. The screams of dying shifters filled the heated air, but Jacob kept blasting at them, too angry, too determined to stop to worry about gases that may be present in the mine.

His brothers stood behind him, gasping in shock at the large red and black scaled creature with a red streak going from the crown of his head down to the tips of his three-pronged tale. Large horn like structures made the tail heavy and powerful and they avoided it as it began to thrash around, threatening to knock the shaft down entirely.

On Jacob went, fire blazing from the nostrils of his horned snout, his orange eyes large and round, gleaming with cold, animalistic hatred until the last scream faded away.

Breathing in once more gave the few that remained a moment to raise a hand. Even in his dragon state Jacob felt pity for these creatures that had given their loyalty to the wrong person. Breathing out, Jacob pushed the pity away. They'd made their choice, as stupid as it may be. They had to go as well, for even after decades in the dark they were still loyal to the man that had put them in their darkness. Once more he breathed in air and blew out fire, watching the last of them disappear into flames, the heat making the room unbearable for those near to it.

Jacob, his brain turning back towards its human side, looked at the pile of ashes and all that remained of the men and women who'd come for him and his brothers, all that was left of decades of hate. The mine was quiet now, the screams done, the sound of thundering feet gone, and Jacob hoped he could forget the sound of it all, the sight of it all, when he laid down to sleep.

A strangled cry of rage came from the room and

Jacob turned, ready to deal death to whoever was stupid enough to come for him now. James was struggling to his feet, gun in hand as he wobbled towards Damesha. Jacob knew he couldn't send a flame into the small room, he'd already pressed his luck sending so much out in a mine that could be filling with methane as they stood there, but more importantly, the women were in there. Turning, he saw Jacqui and Sabrina joining hands as a powerful white beam of energy shot out from the ceiling, Jacqui creating it and Sabrina directing it.

They blasted James first, whatever he was about to scream at them left unsaid as his body exploded into dust from the blasts. Over and over again the light exploded where he'd been before moving on. Each of his co-conspirators took a chance, tried to run, but the women simply weren't having it. Each man disappeared as the blasts of light moved across the floor, the noise almost unbearable as energy exploded inside of the small room. The men had nowhere to run and the screams slowly died away as the women destroyed them one by one. They didn't stop as their gazes locked together, whatever they were creating too powerful to let them loose for the moment. Jacob watched, stunned, as the beam took on a pink hue, blasting the bodies over and over until there was nothing left but the scar the blasts left on the floor.

Allana took off running while everyone was too

stunned to move, escaping down the shaft and aiming for the lower levels. Jacob let her go. He'd seen the fear on her face. She wasn't going to be a problem ever again. He was confident of that.

Jacob thought for a minute that the women would not allow her to leave, kept his ears tilted in the direction she had run and waited for a blast but none came. The women fell apart, their fingers slowly disentangling as their bodies started to fall.

The men shifted back to their human forms and ran for the women, Jacob and Cade catching their mates just as they fainted, their bodies exhausted from the energy they'd just expelled.

"Sabrina. Oh, you beautiful creature you. Come on, you're a vampire, wake up my love." His tone was teasing, a hint of affection in his voice.

Sabrina's eyes blinked open and Jacob began to smile. "There's my girl. Come on, everybody's leaving."

Sabrina got her feet under her and began to look around. "That's it? We're done?"

"It would seem so honey. But we have a few things to discuss, I believe."

Sabrina looked around, dazed at the fact that it was all over. Truly over.

Jacob helped her out of the mine, the others following close behind. Once they reached the forest, Jacob used his skills to take them back to the sanctuary in New Orleans. Jadrian groaned as he saw where he was, his hatred for the place growing now that he knew it was the place where he'd almost fallen into the hands of a traitorous demon.

"Did you really have to bring me back here? Why not send me home? At least there I haven't been humiliated or turned into a shifter, or anything else. Why can't I catch one single break?" He stalked off to be alone, and Jacob let him go.

"Thank you, brother, you saved us all. Including my wife, and for that I'll be eternally grateful." Cade came up to shake his brother's hand.

Jacob realized their roles were reversed, and he was back to being the brother in the shadows. The world shifted again and Jacob stood tall, a king who knew his place.

"It was my duty and my pleasure, brother." He pulled his brother in for a hug, knowing that no matter where they ended up in life, they would always have each other's back.

A few months ago this kind of hug would have made all of them feel awkward, they would have shied away from the contact but now they knew what was most important in life.

"Same from me, Jacob. You have saved me a lot of heartache, and my daughter even more." Kane joined in on the hug, but let his brothers go when Sabrina spoke up.

"I think you two need to feed your wives and put them to bed. We have had quite the experience. Allana flew us to West Virginia in a private jet but then we walked into that mountain and down through the mine for what felt like hours. We deserve some rest." Sabrina looked at the women with sympathy and they looked back with gratitude. She had made two very powerful, lifelong friends in a matter of moments.

Jacob knew relations between vampires and shifters could be strained, but those two women had only just been introduced to the magical world. The magical world was still new to them, an amazement that took their breath away sometimes, but they'd been coping. They'd both tried to include Sabrina in their lives but couldn't hide their fear of her. That was gone now, obliterated the moment they'd all become pawns together.

Jacob took Sabrina to their chamber as his brothers wandered off with their wives. He would have to inform his guards that the world was safe now, that they could stand down, but he still couldn't believe it was all over. He'd spent such a long time now fighting them, waiting for the day when they would be gone that he didn't know what to do now, how to live without fearing them.

"I wish I'd known about Allana sooner," he murmured as they made it to their chamber.

"You can't know absolutely everything, Jacob. You're definitely a smart man and filled with knowledge, but you can't blame yourself for that woman, do you hear me?" She closed the door and pulled him close, brushing her soft, peach-flavoured lips against his. "Would you have taken that man up on his offer to let him live?"

"No, my parents have been dead for a long time." He sighed and stepped away, sinking onto the bed as she followed him, standing between his thighs. "We buried them in our hearts. We knew when they died, we felt it. We don't need to see their remains to accept it. It's not something I really want to see now anyway. It would ruin our memories of them, seeing them like that. We'd remember that and not the good times we had."

"I understand."

She brushed her fingers through his hair, loving the silky texture of the dark strands. Her breasts moved closer to his face and Jacob inhaled her scent.

He needed her but knew that she likely needed some time to settle her nerves. She had been kidnapped, after all, vampire or not. He pushed her back and looked up at her with a smile.

"Would a bath be in order?" He knew she loved a hot bath, the hotter the better.

"I'd love one! And, before you ask, no we weren't

touched by any of the men. We were saved that humiliation at least." She moved away, undoing the metal closures holding her long dark sapphire blue gown together.

"I suppose that's something to be thankful for. I would hate to have to resurrect any of them and kill them again at a much slower pace." He was joking but deep inside he was deadly serious.

He'd known in the mine shaft that he loved her. He might have hated her for turning him, for killing him, but she'd given him an opportunity unlike any other he would ever have in life. And on top of that, she'd offered herself. He'd ignored her since he'd become the king of all magicals, but he wasn't about to let that happen again. There weren't going to be anymore long lonely nights for her, or days spent wondering when she would see him again. Never again.

He went behind the screen to fill the tub, leaving the cold tap off, and went back in to fetch her. She stood wrapped in a robe of white silk with red poppies dotted across it. Her eyes met his, her love clear to see, and Jacob went to his knees in front of her.

"Say you'll be mine for eternity, Sabrina?" He was speaking of more than marriage, more than living together, when he asked her. Jacob knew he'd spend the rest of his life devoted to this beautiful, smart and brave woman.

Sabrina didn't answer him, she went to the tub and got in, flinging her robe over the screen dividing the room.

Jacob's brow scrunched up as he followed her. "Well?"

"Jacob, my darling," she began, but stopped to soap up a sponge to scrub over her skin. "If you have to ask you've not been paying attention."

His feet went out from under him somehow and he landed on a chair just behind him. "What do you mean?"

Fear tightened his stomach. Perhaps she didn't love him, perhaps he'd been a pawn just as much as Jadrian had. Is that what she was telling him?

"Darling, Adrian is gone, off to find his own way in life now. I have released him, he is his own now. Just like you. The moment you took the throne I released you from your tie to me." She was still scrubbing her skin, the pink sponge smoothing down the curves of her calves as she held each one up to wash.

Jacob was distracted for a moment, her pearly white flesh making his mouth go dry as he felt something tighten lower than his stomach. She was perfection, absolute perfection. Her words sank in, though, and he looked at her, even more confused now.

"But, I always know where you are."

"That's because we're soulmates now. Our souls have chosen each other. We may have fights in the future, we may argue and spit at each other, but we're bound together for eternity, my love. I will not be going anywhere without you ever again."

"Oh." So she only loved him because of their nature then?

"No, I love you for you, you obtuse man!" She finally turned and threw the sponge at him, striking him in the head with it before it bounced away. "I love you because you're wonderful, caring, and a death-dealer to those that threaten us. I love you because you make me whole. Something I've never felt in all of my centuries on this planet. Not once. You make me feel as if life is worth living and exploring! Geez!"

Jacob looked at her exasperated expression and went down on his knees in front of her.

"You love me?" He breathed the words, his throat too tight to let him speak.

"Of course I do, you idiot!

He dove into the water, not caring that he soaked the floor or that he was soaking his own clothes, he just wanted to hold her. He'd waited long enough now!

"We'll have to live here, of course, but we can travel too, go wherever you want to go." He was kissing her as he spoke, his lips moving over her face. She was pulling at his clothes, wanting to get him naked.

He assisted her with her removals and pulled her out of the tub, carrying her to the bed, wet hair and all.

"Mm, well, if we are going to spend eternity doing this we had better get started now. Eternity isn't that long, you know?" His mouth came down to hers as they landed on the bed, the passion growing as they moved together.

Not a bad way to end such a massively insane day, he thought.

13

Jadrian

*J*adrian stared into the glass of Scotch he held, thinking he was like the melting ice cube. Almost redundant now, doing more harm by watering the liquor down than chilling it, and better off pulled out of the glass before it ruined the rest of the drink. It was his sixth glass, perhaps it was time to stop.

Glancing up, he decided it was definitely time to stop. He could swear there were two women sitting on the pillow covered floor of the lounge room, making out as their gazes took him in. He squinted, thinking he was probably staring down a potted plant or something, but when he opened his eyes they were still there.

Two months ago he'd have waltzed on over to them,

invited himself for a night of debauchery, but now. Well, Allana had taught him a thing or two. Sometimes the people who acted like they wanted you the most just wanted something from you.

Sure, he'd learned that lesson long ago but he'd thought his judge of character was better than that, he thought he'd learned enough to know when he was being used. Apparently not. She'd taken him for a ride unlike anything he'd ever been on. It did explain why she'd been so hot after Cade and Jacqui but so easily switched to him. She hadn't cared which one she got in with, she just needed an in. Jadrian had given that to her without a second thought. There hadn't been any kind of warning from his gut that something was off about her. The ladies in his family, his brothers that he loved so much, had almost paid the price for him paying more attention to his dick than he did to his head.

Jadrian remembered the way she'd held him after the cave-in in the tunnels but pushed the memory away. So she could fake human compassion, he bet even genocidal dictators occasionally spared a life. Maybe. Cats could eat their young but would defend later litters, so it wasn't like nature didn't allow compassion, even from vile creatures bent on destroying the world. He'd trust a dictator or a baby eating cat more than he'd ever trust Allana again.

He decided to bury his memories, and his dick, in the

two women stripping each other off on the pillow. As he left the bar, someone caught his arm and he turned around to tell them to piss off.

"Cade. I should have known. Man, I don't need the lecture right now. I need to get off and get out of this fucking place." He wasn't slurring his words yet but he was close, his heavy eyelids struggling to stay open.

"I think we need to talk, brother. You're falling apart. It's been a month, I've let you drag yourself through the mud for weeks now. Tonight is the last of it." Cade's voice told Jadrian he didn't expect a response so Jadrian sat down, waiting for the lecture.

"You didn't know. It's that simple. You didn't know who she was, you didn't know her plans, you didn't know she was using you. That's generally the idea of these types of plans, you know? Fool the mark. To be honest, I'm not completely sure your girl was playing for their team." Cade ordered a drink for himself and a coffee for his brother and turned back to Jadrian, who was stunned into silence.

"What do you mean?" Jadrian finally found the ability to speak again and stared at his brother.

"I'm certain that all wasn't as it appeared. I wouldn't be so quick to judge her. Allana was many things but I'm not certain she was a traitor. Even if she did take my wife." Cade's hands tightened but he didn't go on.

"So you think she was working her own angle, trying

to take her father out?" Jadrian sounded hopeful but doubtful. She hadn't been seen since that night, if she was innocent she should have come in and faced the music. Jacob had released a "do not kill" order for her. He seemed to want to give her a trial too, so why hadn't she come in?

Jadrian turned away from his brother, his brain too fuddled at the moment to think too hard about anything. His gaze caught the women again and he forgot about Allana for a moment. A moment that likely wouldn't last but he'd take it.

The brothers silently watched as the two women slowly undressed each other in a corner, as two males brought a woman to a shuddering orgasm in another. Things like that often happened in this lounge and people were free to watch, join, or sit relaxing as they chose. Not something the non-magical world would ever admit to wanting, but Jadrian drunkenly decided they needed more places like it, people needed to get some of those sticks out of their asses and a dick in it instead.

He snorted and almost fell off of his stool.

"Drink your coffee." Cade pushed the cooling liquid to his brother who slurped at it before letting the cup clatter back onto the dish it had been sitting on.

"Look, Cade, you got a wife. A very pregnant wife from the looks of her lately. You're getting laid. I'm not, just fuck off." Jadrian wasn't being his normal careful self now but he knew Cade would forgive him. His heart was broken.

"Actually, since becoming pregnant, Jacqui has become quite adventurous. I had to pull her away from those two last night." Jadrian cracked one eye open and saw Cade was pointing at the women.

"Really?" Jadrian didn't believe him, Cade was drunk!

"Yeah, she was crawling on her hands and knees to them. I had to take her back to our room, and well…" Cade didn't elaborate but he gave Jadrian a look that said he worked his ass off last night.

"Wow. I wanted to know that." Jadrian tried to take Cade's drink but Cade was having none of it.

"Look, Jadrian, I need you to sort your shit, man. Jacob's putting you in charge of Allana's clan. She hasn't surfaced since we sealed the mine shaft off. I have no idea if she's still down there or if she escaped. Maybe she doesn't know about the 'do not kill' order, or that Jacob wants to give her a trial. I do know we can't leave her clan without an Alpha though. You're leaving tomorrow. Get your shit together. Fuck those two or don't, but get your shit together. You have responsibilities and you don't get to run away from them." Cade ordered another drink, asking for an orange juice when he saw his wife enter the room. She was hungrily staring at the two men and women, her gaze going over both

Cade and Jadrian with a sultry hunger that managed to both arouse Cade and set off his jealous mode.

"Fuck, not again. She almost killed me last night." Cade swore under his breath and Jadrian smirked. "You wouldn't believe she was a virgin when we got married. Now she simply can't get enough of sex and she wants to explore it all. It's just sex, I am not a jealous kind of guy and wouldn't mind, but I want her to make decisions on her good sense, not her hormones. Fuck, this being pregnant thing is going to kill me. Luckily, she's going as quick as Damesha did."

"Man, I don't know if I envy you that or not." Jadrian looked back at his coffee as his sister-in-law walked up, trying not to giggle.

"Hey, baby." Jacqui, normally a bit reserved in public, snuggled up to Cade's side, still standing as she ran a finger down his neck, her eyes hungry for him.

Jadrian noted her stomach had grown a bit more in the hours since he'd seen her last and knew he could very well be an uncle again by the end of the week.

"Wait, what?" Jadrian's brain was sluggish and he had just processed the words about being Alpha and going to Allana's tribe. "I'm not going to a rainforest, Cade. It's always raining in Louisiana. Fuck that!"

Cade turned, grinning at his brother. "Not my decision, brother. You moped around and Jacob decided to give you something to do."

Jadrian glared at his empty coffee mug, how the hell was he going to get out of this shit?

"I don't want to go to the swamp. It fucking rains!" He pushed the cup away, and stood up unsteadily. "I'm going to talk to Jacob."

"No, you're not. Go to bed, get your stuff packed, and go. You'll be good at this, Jadrian. You just need to sober up and you'll see. Go on now, off to bed."

Jadrian glared at his brother once more and wobbled off. This was bullshit. The fucking swamp. He was going to talk to Jacob. But he didn't, he went to his room as Cade told him to and passed out instead.

* * *

Jacob

"SHE'S NEW." Jacob looked at the redhead and remembered Allana for a moment. The two were totally different, though. This one's hair wasn't as shiny, her face wasn't as perfect. She was lovely though, and a volunteer. He felt himself going hard as he looked at his partner, the woman that was far more than his wife. She was his queen now.

"She tastes of blueberries and maple syrup." Sabrina went back to the vein she'd been nursing in the woman's bared neck.

Naked, the women were on the bed, waiting for Jacob to join them. Gulping slowly he decided to watch them for a bit. This was sex, plain and simple, and though he hadn't fucked anyone but Sabrina, he did enjoy the nights when they shared a volunteer.

"Strip, darling, and get up here beside of her." Sabrina patted the blood red duvet and Jacob couldn't say no.

He was already aching for her, aching for the blood that would nurture him, and let his clothes fall to the floor. He strode to the bed on strong legs, his entire body well developed and he knew it when Sabrina gave him an appreciative look. The volunteer, nameless for now, was too enraptured in Sabrina's fingers on her nipples to notice he was there.

"Our king wants to join us, Liza, is that alright?" Sabrina prompted, needing the woman's consent before Jacob would touch her.

"Yes, please, touch me. Oh fuck, please touch me." The experience of giving blood to vampires was highly erotic for humans and could become an addiction in itself. Liza was new but loving it already.

"He won't fuck you, my lovely, but I will." Sabrina's slim fingers trailed down the woman's flat stomach, down her bare pubis, disappearing into her folds. Jacob's heart sped up as he watched, knowing Sabrina had just entered her when Liza's eyes opened wide and lost.

Liza gave a ragged moan and Jacob moved, his tongue finding her very pale pink nipple. Not as large as Sabrina's, not as firm, but still delightful. His tongue rasped the tip and Liza began to purr. Jacob's fangs pierced the woman's skin gently, still drawing on her nipple, a delight he had found human women couldn't resist. Many of them exploded as soon as his fangs pierced their skin, others took a bit of coaxing.

Jacob thought this was one of the more challenging volunteers and moaned, pressing his cock into her slim hip, coaxing her to explore him, to explore his queen. He felt her hand flutter down, heard her gasp as she felt him, and watched her, the taste of her blood making him harder.

Sabrina did her own bit of purring and Jacob glanced at her. Liza's fingers were moving between Sabrina's thighs, diving in and out of her. Sabrina must be very wet, Jacob could smell her unique scent and craved her taste. He decided it could wait, the volunteer's body was going tense as Jacob's fingers joined Sabrina in the blood donor's folds, pressing inside of her. He matched his pace to the pace she'd set with Sabrina, to the pace she'd set with him. For a moment he wasn't sure who was touching who, or who was supposed to be coming, he was lost in the scent of the women, in the taste of the blood, of the incredible feeling of having his cock stroked while he and his queen got their volunteer off.

He wanted to fall back and enjoy the moment, let the women pamper him, but he knew he shouldn't ask until he gave some pleasure himself. He loved his queen, there was no doubt about that, but when there was mutual agreement and mutual enjoyment, sex with others could be fun. Even if he hadn't technically penetrated anyone but Sabrina.

That was his own rule and one he had no intention of breaking. He hadn't met a woman worthy of it yet, and doubted he ever would. There was only one Sabrina, after all.

With an aching dick, Jacob moved away from the woman as she opened her eyes, filled with wonder. Her hands had slowed to a halt as she came down from her high and her hips had stopped thrashing. Now she looked at Sabrina. His queen leaned over to kiss the woman and Jacob saw her tongue sliding along the other woman's.

Sabrina was a romantic at heart and had lit candles all over their chamber. The flames caused lights to flicker over her body, shadows forming and disappearing. He wanted to follow the light patterns with his tongue. He moved over her and the woman did the same, coming to life when Jacob moved.

The volunteer moved over Sabrina's face, her thighs embracing Sabrina's head, and Jacob caught a faint giggle as Sabrina's arms came up to clasp the woman's ass, pulling her closer. Jacob wondered if Sabrina would feed from the woman that way as well. The image made Jacob harder, and he ground his dick into the bed, needing some kind of relief, even if it was temporary.

He needed to bury himself in his partner, he needed her heated walls around him, but he wouldn't take until he had given. Not even a little bit.

Jacob wasn't sure why he was losing control tonight, but he knew he needed to contain it. He couldn't lose control.

With a low growl, he grazed her clit with his teeth and felt her buck beneath him. He could drink from her, but the experience would definitely send him over a precipice he didn't want to cross tonight. Not yet, at least. He didn't care what happened after Sabrina got off, they could walk out of the room or turn him into their sex slave, but first she would get off.

He heard Liza whimper above him, the sound turning into a low moan as her back arched and her hips began to move on Sabrina's face. Jacob smiled, wondering if he could distract Sabrina. He let his teeth graze her once more as his fingers slid into her wet confine. When he brushed his tongue against her clit, pressing it into the nub, her hips jerked, pressing the organ into his mouth.

Jacob sucked her clit hard and fast, knowing that he

was going to have to fuck her, that he wanted it too much but he didn't move. She had to get off first.

The blood volunteer started to shudder as he pressed another finger into Sabrina, stretching her, preparing her for him. Sabrina's hips swiveled beneath him as he slid the fingers, three of them now, in and out of her, his pace teasingly slow, achingly slow, until she was throbbing with tension. Almost there.

He sucked his way off her clit and spoke loud enough for her to hear over the keening cries of the volunteer.

"I'm going to fuck you so hard when you're done with her. I'm going to get my cock so far up in this pussy that you won't know where you end and I begin, sweetness." Then he went back to clit, his tongue flicking at the button, stabbing at it, until she let go and threw the woman off, her fingers buried in his hair as she rode his tongue.

He fucked her hard with his fingers, knowing she liked an edge of pain to her pleasure. It always got her off hard when he gave her just the biting hint of pain.

Sabrina's back edged off the bed and the pair began to rise together as her body started to contract around him, her thighs encircled his head, matching the grasping suction of her pussy. Jacob went with it, not letting up on her as she went higher and higher, her body a writhing snake he could barely hang on to. She had really let go tonight.

His tongue toyed with her clit, the swelling organ fascinating him as she exploded, words falling from her lips that only he could understand, the tongue was so ancient.

"Fuck me, Jacob, oh baby, take me please." She begged for his cock and he was more than willing to give it. He turned her, her legs opening for him as she hung suspended in the air. His cock nudged her opening, but he wanted to tease her. His left hand found her hip, pulling her to him and Jacob stroked her with the head of his cock, needing to hear more from her.

"How do you want it, baby? Tell me." He edged the head into her opening, barely more than centimeters inside of her. She tried to move, to thrust down onto him, but he held her still with his hand on her hip. "No baby, tell me how you want it."

"I want it hard, Jacob. Give it to me hard. Fuck my pussy until I can't beg you for anymore. Please!"

Her naughty words thrilled him, made his toes curl, and he pushed a fraction deeper into her, despite wanting to be buried balls deep in her walls.

"Do you want me to tell you how good it feels to fuck you, Sabrina? How I love having my cock in you?"

"Yes! Tell me!" she panted, struggling to remain still but his other hand was in her hair now, holding her head up so he could see her face, even though she couldn't see him.

"I wouldn't leave if I didn't have to. I have the filthiest fantasies about you when I should be working on budgets. I remember how you clench around me, your pussy clamping down like the greedy little monster it is. It's a wonder I get anything done, thinking about you and this oh so fuckable pussy of yours, Sabrina."

Her eyes, visible to him as he pulled her head around, were glazed with her need, with the pleasure he was giving her, and he knew she needed a little more to go over the edge once more. He'd go with her this time.

"Maybe tomorrow I'll take you to that lounge room. The fuck room and fuck you in front of everyone. Let them see how eager you are for it, how much you love my dick." His words weren't about exploitation or humiliation, they were about getting Sabrina off. He knew she had a thing for public fucking, on top of everything else.

Telling her he was going to take her in public made her walls clamp down harder than he'd felt before and Jacob gave her just a little bit more of his cock as she mewled out a plea for more.

"Oh but baby, you haven't even got the audience hard yet. They're just sitting there, salivating over those fabulous tits of yours, wanting to suck those dark nipples. Fuck they're sweet." He thrust a little deeper, her dripping pussy taking every wide inch of him greedily. He could feel her walls trying to urge him deeper, trying to milk him deeper inside of her, but he held himself back, not letting himself go just yet.

"Maybe I'll have you on your knees first, taking my cock between those pouty lips of yours. They're so fabulously dirty, you know? I thought about them while jerking off in my office one night. You were asleep, exhausted, and I didn't want to wake you so I went in there and thought about those lips and… ohhhhh!" He had to stop himself as he felt a shudder go down his spine, a shudder that went straight down his dick and into her. He watched as the muscles of her back responded, shivering the way his had.

"More, Jacob, more. Tell me more." She panted the words, controlling herself a little better now.

"You'd take my cock out, and wrap those lips around the head, sucking me until my knees buckled. Then you'd swallow the rest of me, swallowing me straight down your throat."

A little deeper, and Jacob had to suck in a deep breath. So fucking tight. So fucking gorgeous. And all his.

"You'd be such a good girl, Sabrina, you'd take me there in front of all of those people watching, you'd take your king's cock like the good girl you are."

One more thrust and every centimeter of his flesh was buried inside her. He paused as he took in the sensation of her pussy fluttering around him, her walls working him without either of them moving.

"Fuck you're good, Sabrina." He breathed the words as he pulled her up to a position where his cock was banging into her g-spot.

"Jacob!" She cried out his name, reaching behind her to grasp his hips.

"That's it, baby, ride my dick." He let her move, let her have her way with him, until they were both covered in a sweaty film from their exertions.

A glance down at the bed below them showed the volunteer had her eyes glued to them, her hands between her own legs as she pleasured herself. Jacob gave her a wink and thrust into Sabrina, giving her the wild ride she'd asked for, at last. Bending her forward, he fucked into the queen, his length stroking every inch of her inner walls.

The girl stood, steadied herself, and pulled Sabrina down to her face, tongue out and sucking before Sabrina even realized what was happening.

"They can look all they want, Sabrina, they can lick you, they can touch you, but I'm the only one that gets to fuck you. I'm the only one that gets that little bit of heaven. Mine." He growled the words as he felt her insides start to quiver, and he worked his cock just a little deeper, claiming her.

"Yours, Jacob, only yours!" She agreed with a sob of pleasure as her body went rigid around him.

Jacob let go then, his hips flying as he fucked into her, Liza's tongue flying on Sabrina's clit, the royal couple spiraling in the air, Liza with them, as they flew with each other to a place where they rippled, where they shot, where pleasure was the only thing that existed.

Jacob gave her everything he had and she gave the same in return. A unit, one.

"I love you." He croaked the words in her ear as he came back to the real world, his emotions finally freed.

"I love you, Jacob." She whispered back. "For now and always."

He knew she meant it, he knew she'd fight with him for eternity, for their right to claim each other. This was the real thing and though she might have to destroy him to create this new world of theirs, he knew she had not been wrong. Brave, foolish, perhaps even insane, but the gamble had been worth it to experience this, to feel this.

She'd taken his old life away but she'd given him an entirely new world and they would face it together. Jacob had lived his entire life in the shadows of his brothers, of his parents, of who and what he was. He'd been happy in those shadows, never truly wanting any more than what he had. A quiet, calm man, he'd been content with his lot in life. Sabrina had changed all that. She'd brought him into the very public life, she'd given him power far beyond anything he could have ever imagined because she thought he could save the world. So far, she'd proven herself right.

They'd won the battle against the Mungons, the magical world was at peace now, or as peaceful as it could be where magicals were involved. He had the world in the palm of his hand and he was already casting his gaze in the direction of the non-magical world, looking for ways to make the lives of the masses better without their knowledge. Most of all she'd given him love, the one thing neither had truly counted on.

What started as a bid to save their way of life had turned into a battle of wills but now they'd truly won it all. They would always win as long as they were together. The vampire queen and her vampire dragon-shifter king, forever.

Jadrian

She hadn't loved me, she hadn't wanted me, she'd only been after a goal. The words played over and over in my mind, my stupid, addled mind.

"Jadrian! You ready?" I turned as I heard my brother's voice, worried and concerned. Still.

"I am, Cade. Let's go." Cade was going with me to the chopper taking me back to the swampy home of Allana's clan. I was their Alpha now.

I looked around the monastery one last time, my senses reaching out for her.

Allana.

I closed my eyes, taking in the smell of the place, hoping stupidly that I might catch her scent.

Nothing.

With a ragged sigh, I turned away, admitting defeat finally.

"You know she's your mate, right? That's why you're taking this so hard." Cade looked at me with pity in his eyes and I almost forgot what he'd said. My eyes narrowed as I stared my brother down.

"My mate?" That couldn't be true, I would be dead after being separated from my mate for so long.

"Think back, brother. Did you feel an odd surge of heat go down your spine, something weird and freaky?" He paused, thinking. "This obsession you have with her, the way you can't stop thinking about her?"

He came close to me, his fist digging into a spot in my abdomen. "It hurts here, right? Aches and burns and nothing makes it better, right?"

"How… do you know that?" I rubbed my hand over the spot, annoyed that he was right.

"Because that's what happens when your soul decides on its mate, you dumb fuck!" Cade grinned at him, easing the sting of his words. "She isn't too far away, just not close either."

"Still, what killed Mom and Dad then? They were only separated by a few dozen feet!" Jadrian hated reminding his brother of their parents but it was his only example.

"I think it's because you were made a shifter." Cade

looked certain as he stepped away and the helicopter's blades began to whirl.

"Right. Too much to think about. I'll have cell service out there in the swamp, right?" I looked at the chopper, uncertain. I just wanted to go back to Kansas, forget all this shit, and go back to my normal life.

"You're going to make a great Alpha, Jadrian. Just remember, *you're* the Alpha now. Don't take anybody's shit and put down dissent quickly, understand?" Cade's dark eyes bored into mine. "And call me, I'll be there in an instant if you need me. Jacob didn't make a stupid decision, stop doubting yourself." He looked sure enough to convince me for now so I hugged him and left him there wordlessly, my bag clutched in my hands.

The helicopter flew me to a deeper part of the bayou, the special pontoons allowing us to land in water 40 minutes later. I looked around as a pirogue came out to join us. A woman with blonde hair greeted me.

"Come on in, sha, I'll take you over." She was pointing at the thirty or so buildings on stilts behind her. How the fuck was I supposed to get out of this place?

The houses looked well-maintained. There were boats floating under the houses that looked like they were kept in proper running order, and smiling faces on each porch. That wasn't the problem, the problem was a lack of roads and road signs. I didn't even know where I was. Jacob had well and truly dropped me in the shit.

"I guess there isn't much choice… sha." I grinned at the twenty-something woman, a little on the thick side, and managed to get into the small boat without tipping us over. I dropped my bag in the bottom and she started to push the pole in her hands, guiding us to the largest building.

All of the houses and buildings were connected by a running pier-system, sidewalks in a world with ground beneath them. Out here, several feet of water could pass under the houses before it even touched them.

"This one's yours, sha. Go on now, climb up that there ladder. You go on first." Her words were kind of sing-songy and out of sequence but I found it charming.

She shouted something I couldn't understand up to the people staring down at us and they all smiled and waved. Somebody caught my bag as I threw it up on the pier and climbed over.

"Hi," I said simply, staring at the gathered faces. Young and old, blonde hair and black, even a bit of red, male and female, there must have been over a hundred people staring at me around the complex.

"Hi!" An older man came out of the assembled people and took my hand to shake it. "Welcome. Let's get you settled in. I'm Alton, I'm the accountant around here. I guess I'll play the guide for now." He took me into the large building, the first floor just a large open room, a living room in front, kitchen in the back, and a couple of closets. A fireplace sat in a corner of the living room, untouched for now.

It sank in that I was now the Alpha for these people and I looked around. What could I say to them? Allana's home, now my home, was overwhelming in its comforts and the expectant faces behind me left me speechless.

"Well, I... I guess I should introduce myself. I'm Jadrian Alexander, your new Alpha." I paused as quiet murmurs of approval filled the air. "I'm new to this so I guess we'll learn together, shall we?"

"You hungry, sha?" the blonde girl asked. "We made a gumbo and some rice for you. It being your first day here, well, we thought we'd let you rest." She grinned at me.

"Thank you. What's your name?" I stared down at her, realizing then I was taller than all of them.

"Ruby, sha. Nice to meet ya." She held her hand out and then everybody got in a line and did the same, telling me their names, who they belonged to, which children were theirs, and letting me know what they did.

My head was spinning by the time the end of the line came and a woman with red hair stood before me with a bowl of rice and gumbo in her hands.

I stared at her, realizing now that the ache had disappeared, that my depression had lifted the moment we landed, and that I'd been too distracted by it all to notice. I felt better because my mate was here and I'd missed it. Already failing at noticing what was going on around me, for fuck's sake!

"Allana." I hadn't dared hope she'd be here. I hadn't allowed myself to hope to find her, but there she was.

"Cade sent me here. He said Jacob was sending you." She was thinner, her face a little wild, and her hair had lost some of its luster. She was suffering.

Allana turned as I absorbed her words, telling the people something and they all trailed out, happily talking with each other. Cade. He'd sent her here. That bastard knew and hadn't told me. I felt anger surge through me but it quickly disappeared.

"What happened, Allana? Explain everything to me, please." I went to the couch, a long wooden high-backed bench with dark brown cushions, handmade from local wood it looked like. I set the bowl she'd given me on a table that was definitely hand-carved, and looked at her.

She sat beside me, tucking a foot under her bottom. Pushing her hair out of her face she looked stressed, overwhelmed, and an urge to ease her burden filled me. I told it to fuck off until I had some answers.

"You know *he* was my father, and that I brought the Alexander women to him. I did it to draw you all together, to end this. I didn't do it to betray any of you."

Her blue eyes caught mine, pleading with me for understanding. "It was stupid, desperate, but this needed to end and I knew only the Alexanders could stop my father. He was... ruthless. To everyone, including me."

I felt myself thawing a bit. She must have explained everything to Cade, he must have believed her for her to still be alive. "Alright. Go on."

"When I was still little more than a cub he threw me out, told me to sink or swim. If I learned to swim he told me to come back. He didn't have a use for female cubs, you see." Her eyes were defiant as she spoke, sparking with life and the beauty that had so captivated me.

"Did you go back?" She must have, I knew, she'd arranged to take our women.

"I called him to arrange the meeting. I didn't see him, he'd have probably seen through me before I could pull it all off." She looked guilty for a moment and I knew it was because of the danger she'd put the women in.

"I don't think they were in much danger, Allana. Did you see what they did to him?" I could still remember the sound of the blasts and the light from the surging energy Sabrina had created and Jacqui had directed.

"I know, but if they hadn't been who they were... fuck." She stood up, pacing around her own home. I saw now the little touches she'd added, paintings of local wildlife and flowers, cushions and plants, even the furniture was something I could tell she'd picked herself.

In that moment the anger, the disbelief, all of it slid away. "And me? Where do I fit into all of this?"

"Jadrian, I…" Her words trailed off as she stopped pacing. "You were a complication I wasn't expecting."

Her words hit me like a wrecking ball. "So you weren't just," I twirled my hands, looking for the words, "using me? You weren't just trying to get me to give you information, or to turn me to your father's side?"

"Never, Jadrian!" She came to me on her knees, her hands taking mine as she stared up at me. "I really like your brother's wife, and yeah, I'd have slept with them both, but the minute I laid eyes on you, Jadrian. You rocked me to the core!"

I looked down at her, remembering another time when she was between my legs, her lips doing very naughty things. I wouldn't let my desire rule me.

"You didn't turn me on purpose?" The memory of my first humiliating shift came back to me and I looked away from her.

"No, and I certainly didn't turn you into a duck shifter." Her smile could not be repressed and honestly, I can't blame her. That shit had been funny and I'd have laughed if it had been anyone else. "Well, I didn't mean to. And if I'm not mistaken, you can turn into more than that now, can't you?"

I shifted around on the couch, for some reason all of my anger and distrust had fled, along with my pain. I watched her for a moment, seeing her hair gradually lift back into life, and the hollows under her eyes disappeared. She was the beautiful woman I'd been longing for, the one I thought I'd never see again.

"Yeah, I can change into a few things now. Allana." I caught her chin in my fingers, staring into her eyes. "Where do we go from here? What happens now?"

She looked uncertain for a moment but I knew she felt the spark where I touched her chin. I saw it in her eyes. I also saw desire flaring into life.

"We do whatever we want to. Jacob's putting out the word that I'm free to go. You're the Alpha now so I guess it's your choice. I'm just a subject." She'd lost a lot in her bid to free us all from the plotting of the Mungons, more than I'd realized.

It all came crashing down on me and I pulled her into my arms at last, wanting to comfort her, wanting to open that crack of pain I'd seen in her and let it all out so I could replace it with nothing but happiness.

She sobbed as I pulled her head down to my shoulder, her arms wrapping around me. I felt it then, that feeling of truly being home, of being someone's mate. Her mate.

I held her through it all, through the wailing, through the explanation of a lifetime of being an evil man's daughter, of her fear of failing in her own plot against him. And then there was me. She'd truly felt something for me and she'd known I was her mate.

"I didn't know until I left, not for sure, but when the pain started I knew. I came back here, it was tolerable here, and I could deal with it. But I don't know how long I'd have lasted, Jadrian. If you'd left the moment you saw me I think I'd have died." I wiped away her tears, fighting back my own, handing her a tissue from a box on the table.

"I'm an idiot, Allana. A total idiot. 'I didn't know' isn't much of an excuse but I had no idea our souls had mated until Cade told me earlier." I took a deep breath, blinking the tears away. "I stopped thinking you were evil a while back, but I had no idea how to find you, or even if you wanted to be found."

"I needed to think, to get my own head straight. Then Cade told me what was going on. I knew just showing up wasn't going to work. This is what he and Jacob came up with." She gave me a watery smile, and an awareness of how she was nestled into my lap hit us both.

Her eyes searched mine as she wound her arms around my neck, her mouth getting closer. "Jadrian?"

"Kiss me, Allana." I wanted the feisty hell-cat I'd known back, this soft, broken woman was too much to bear, too unlike the real woman I knew. I prodded her into taking back some of her self-confidence by feeding her an order.

She did as she was told but she did it with a fierce growl of satisfaction. She moved, straddling me, locking our groins together as her lips pressed into mine.

Frantic need took control of us both and we tore clothes away until we were naked in each other's arms. I held my arms up against her back, leaning her away from me as I kissed her. Long hair trailed over my arms, silky and sultry. Her nude skin was a temptation I couldn't resist and I began to explore her, tasting her neck and shoulders before I trailed down to her breasts.

Peach colored nipples puckered under my tongue and her inhalation of breath was my reward. I felt her gasp all the way to my throbbing cock. She wanted me. I gave her what she needed.

Her fingers buried in my hair, pulling at it as she gripped my head, pressing me into her breast.

I felt her long, slim fingers trails down my bare back, her nails scratching my skin as she lost herself in my touch.

"Don't stop, Jadrian. I've missed you so much. Touch me more, please, more." I let my hands trace down her back, feeling her own muscles, down to her firm ass, grasping at her there as she began to move against me. I kneaded her bottom close to her center, my fingers grazing the most intimate parts of her.

"Come on, Allana, you know we don't get what we want until we've spent the night exploring. Didn't I tell you that?" She pulled back, confused, but then she gave me that sexy grin.

"Ah, yes, I remember." She pulled away from me. "We have to be thorough, begging each other, on the verge of dying. Don't we?"

Kneeling on the floor she took me in her mouth, my thick head passing her lips, and sliding easily down her throat. I stroked her neck absently, gasping as she swallowed me, focused on the intense pleasure of her mouth on my dick.

Her hands explored my thighs, wound up to my mouth, and a slim finger pushed between my lips. I sucked at it, mimicking her actions below, loving the taste of her. I pulled it away, winding my fingers with hers.

"Don't you dare make me come, Allana. Not yet." I pulled her head away when she began to suck harder, faster, her head bobbing in a blur on me.

"Jadrian! Please? I want to taste you." Her eyes were alluring, and I wanted to fall into them, to let her suck me off, but I couldn't do it. I wanted to know what it felt like to be held inside of her.

"Later, babe." I turned her, walking away. I went to a fridge and pulled out a pitcher of tea. I stared at her on the couch, pouting so fucking prettily, as I guzzled down the tea I'd poured. "Savor it, Allana."

I ran a hand down my side and over my stomach, watching as she watched me. She spread her long, muscular legs, the legs of a runner, and let me see her secrets. She was wet, so wet, and her fingers found her clit quickly as her eyes dared me to resist her. I grinned at her, leaning back against the counter, sucking down tea like I wasn't about to spill all over the floor.

My long frame wasn't easy to perch nonchalantly on the counter but I managed as Allana opened her sex, stroking herself into a moan as she watched me for any sign of cracking.

"You're going to make yourself come, Allana. And what are you going to do when I'm not there to clench around? You know how that's going to feel, right? My cock buried balls deep inside of you, all of me, as you clench into a screaming orgasm?" I stared at her smugly, a grin of my own capturing her attention.

"Then you'd best come over here, Jadrian and stop fucking with me." Her eyes went wide for a moment as I shifted, but I was only repositioning myself. I set the glass of tea down now that it was empty and took myself in hand instead.

"Is this what you want? This hard cock, all for you. You want it in that slick pussy of yours, filling you up." I moved closer, standing just in front of the table at the couch.

I could smell her scent, luring me to her. I had to taste her.

I dropped to my knees between her legs, pressing her thighs open when she tried to clamp them shut. I swiped at her with my tongue, from bottom to top, going back somewhere around center to lap up her juices. My head exploded, and a buzzing started in my ears.

I lapped at her, trying to lick her dry but I only made her wetter, her hips moving to follow my tongue, to catch me when I reached her clit and hold me still. Her fingers dragged through my hair, holding me in place as she rode my tongue.

I pulled away as she started to pant my name, wanting to be inside of her so desperately it fucking hurt. "Not yet, Allana, not yet baby."

I moved, sitting up to take my cock and guide it to her opening. I watched, gasping myself, as I felt the tip meet her wet flesh. Then it disappeared, slid in, and I stopped. I wanted to plunge into her but I wanted to savor this more.

Her hips tilted and another inch of me disappeared, an inch of thick flesh that made me grit my teeth in pleasure. I pressed a little further and she was taking five inches of me. I thought I'd lose it then but I held back.

I looked into her eyes, her feet flat on the floor, and waited, holding my breath until that point when her eyes flared. Then I let her take the last five inches, sinking down into her. She wrapped her legs around my waist, sealing us together, taking every centimeter of me she could get.

I groaned, unable to form words as we began to move together. I couldn't get enough traction so I pulled her up and took her to the nearest wall, keeping her wrapped around me.

I braced her there, holding her ass as I began a brutal, pounding pace that had us both panting against each other's mouths, our lips tangling just to let go a moment later as she began to explode. That first pulse triggered me and we exploded together, our bodies pressing together, sweat causing us to slide easily with each other.

Her head fell back as she came and I watched her face, I watched her pleasure, and followed, staring down at her in adoration, in total awe. I felt the world rock as I came, her body pulsing around me, taking me deeper, stealing my words again as I emptied into her greedy body.

"Mine." I gasped against her forehead as she slid down my body, too relaxed to hang on any longer.

"Mine." Her eyes met mine and I knew I'd found my mate.

"Together we're going to run this clan, Allana, you by my side. My eternal mate. Together we'll keep the shifter world safe, we'll keep our clan safe."

"Yes, Jadrian. Together." Her arms wound around mine. "But for now, I want round two. I'm a bit concerned."

I kissed the tip of her nose and grinned down at her. "And why is that?"

"Well," she said, kissing my chin as she did her own grinning. "I thought fucking you would get you out of my system. It seems to have had the opposite effect."

Her hands slid down my sides and around to my ass, pulling me into her stomach. "That's a bad thing?"

"Not being able to get enough of you? Yeah, that could be a problem! We have a clan to cater to." Her lips were running over my chest and I knew I wouldn't be seeing anyone else today.

"Later, so much later. Where's the bedroom in this place?" I laughed with her as I carried her up the stairs and into a bedroom decorated with a deep red and black. Lovely, but all I was interested in was the large bed.

I dropped her there and followed her down, my golden skin covering her pale white.

"I'm going to write songs for you, I'm going to write books about you," I told her as I traced my lips down her throat, my fingers exploring her hips.

"I'm going to paint you naked on our bed, in a pirogue, on a swamp bank tempting in naïve young maidens, or maybe in that bathtub." That piqued my interest, what was so special about it, but her fingers started to trail down my face, and over my lips.

"I think we're going to be very busy." I gasped when she kissed me, letting her take my thoughts away.

The war was over, she hadn't been betraying us, and for now, there was peace. I settled between her thighs, missing the text message from Cade saying that Jacqui was in labor. Later I'd see it and we'd go to see our new niece. Anastasia Stella Alexander was born on the day my life became unimaginably wonderful. That had to be a good thing, right?

ANNIE

———

We never ask to be born, we just are. Humans, dogs, snakes, none of us ask for the life we are given or the road we are put on, we just are. My life was a little more difficult than most, because I was born into a world where dogs aren't always seen as living, breathing, *thinking* creatures, we only exist.

Sometimes, that existence puts us on the streets in one land where we are abused, taken to kill shelters then rescued. And then, sometimes, only sometimes, we are rescued and put into a van after terrible things have happened, things that make us afraid of what's coming next. I shivered in a van for several days, though I was treated well, because I'd come to expect the bad things life has to offer, I'd come to expect pain.

This time though, when the van stopped for good

and I was let out of my kennel, something new happened. Instead of a city full of noise, with kicking feet and screaming faces, I was greeted by rolling green hills, quiet, and a face filled with amazement and love. I envied whoever the lady was looking at, and kept my head down, my tail tucked between my legs. Pain was always possible, as was hunger if I did something wrong.

When the lady took my lead, I couldn't help it, I was so afraid of being let down again, that my bladder let go and I could not move. I could not tell her of my fears, I could not tell her why I was so afraid, and I feared a kick for that. I feared a new life of being screamed at. I feared more hunger. I feared a life without love, though I wasn't really sure what love was.

Was love the way my mommy took care of me when I was little, sacrificing her own nutrition for mine? Was it the way some of the ladies at the last shelter had saved me from the kill station? I don't know, I'm not sure I actually remember what it even *feels* like. For now, I was terrified, because once again, I'd peed on something, though I think this is the stuff humans calls grass. I've never felt it so I don't know. I do know what kicks feel like and I shifted, trying to make myself so small.

That did not happen though, for something even more amazing happened. The lady actually *bent down to pet me!*

Pet me!

"It's okay, Annie, we'll take *your* time honey." I looked up at her, my body shivered and the scent of fear filled the air. I hated that scent but I could not help that either. I didn't know what the lady was saying, her words came out odd, but there was kindness in them, and something soft that made me feel warm inside, despite the cold in the air.

"You have a new home, I'm going to take you there now. Can I pick you up?" Gently she put an arm under my belly, that place where so much pain had happened a few months ago and was still sore, so I skittered away.

"It's okay." She soothed me with a hand on my head, smoothing down my fur.

Again, she put her arm under me, but lower, and picked me up. I didn't know what to do so I kept still, didn't move, and looked around. We were going to another car. She put me inside and then we were moving, but this time I could see out, even though I was too afraid to look. I stayed low in the seat, my fear too great.

And then I was at a home, and there was a lady and a man waiting for me. I was taken inside and the women spoke for a little while as I stayed glued to my place on the couch. There was something wrong with the new lady. She needed a protector, and for the first time in my life I wanted to be the one that did that.

She came to site beside me, her gentle hand learning

my body, petting me as she spoke gentle words that made me sleepy. M y head ended up in her lap somehow and before long I was asleep. When I woke up she was surrounding me, holding me, whispering more of those strange meaningless sounds as the nightmare that had woke me finally let me go. I swiped her hand with my tongue, learning her taste, and then put my head back down.

It took a few months but I finally came to know what the lady was saying, and that when the sound "ann-nee" came out she was calling me. She called me often, and I loved her for it. I slept at her feet, or by her side, the man giving up his place behind her back to offer me more protection in the night. I often had nightmares but they were going now, as this new warm feeling that filled me from them chased the bad memories away.

I had treats, and walks, toys, and comfort when the thunder monsters came to shake the floor. My food and water came in bowls that the humans often filled, I learned about television and music. Music was glorious and I loved it. The woman was glorious too and I did not like to be away from her for too long.

She was my best friend, and sometimes she was ill, but I'd always be there for her, to make sure she was okay and to get the man if she needed him. I liked him too, but there was something about the woman, something that made me want to be around her. She was beautiful, even if I was bad and couldn't hold my bladder.

For the first few months, I could only go for walks on a lead, but I loved to run. Sometimes my humans would take me to a park and let me run, and I couldn't help it. I'd dash around, always running back to her, but running, running as fast as my legs and my heart would let me. It wasn't as good as being with the woman but boy was it close.

One day we moved, to a place not far away and something incredible happened. One day the door opened but it did not shut. I made a dash for it, running and running until I could run no more, but the humans let me. That's when I figured out how to do something the humans called "sploring". I'd sniff and run, do some more sniffing and some more running, but always coming back home to make sure they were still there.

That's when my freedom really began. I could run when I wanted to, without a lead, or worries. I made new doggy friends and we'd go around, playing and running. Until that day.

We found some chicken in a bowl, sitting out in the open, and we all had some. We weren't hungry but as street dogs, former in my case, we took food when it was presented. Afterwards, we all got really hot, and kind of sick feeling so I left, and crawled into bed with my human. She wasn't feeling too good either, but I needed her.

She stroked me as I began to pant uncontrollably, and when my eyes rolled back in my head and I couldn't breathe, she took me to a thing called a vet. I tried, I tried so hard, I kicked my legs, I tried to get up, but there was something wrong. The vet man said a word like poy-son, and before long, the world went dark as I heard the woman screaming.

I didn't want to leave her, I just had to. I was drawn away like a leaf on the wind, blown away from the only love I'd known.

"Annie. Wake up, Annie." I tried to open my eyes, I thought I had, but I could not see anything but a pinprick of light. "Hi there, Annie. I'm sorry to meet you under such sad circumstances, but it can't be helped."

"Where am I? What is the place? I want my human!" Somehow the voice seemed to understand me and for a moment the light grew brighter.

"I'm sorry, Annie, the woman is of a time forgotten now. You won't see her again."

"But she needs me! I protect her. I love her!" I panicked, trying to move, but I couldn't.

"Annie, you are star-child, you can only go forward, not backward. There is a new time for you. And a new place. This one won't be so bad though. I promise you that. The humans did not treat you well in your last life.

This time, I'll make sure myself you have a better chance."

"A better chance at what?" I wanted to go back to the woman but I couldn't. My heart broke and I wanted to howl, but had no lungs to do it with.

"A better chance at life, Annie. A better chance to show the humans how to love."

I didn't like it, I wanted the human called mommy. I tried to glare at the light but couldn't.

"You can stay here if you prefer. Be amongst the stars."

"Would I have a body?" My voice shook, I didn't like the sound of that being a star bit

"No, you'd be like me, little more than light."

"No! I want to run! I have to run, it's what I do!" My voice was panicked, a deep fear making my voice shake even more. "Why can't I just go back to my Mommy?"

"I'm sorry, Annie, it's impossible." He sounded even more sad and I wanted to scream in anger and hurt but knew it would get me nowhere.

"Fine! I'm not going to like it though and you can't make me! I want Mommy!"

I heard a sound like a sigh, and something that sounded like a sniffle, but then I was on a brightly lit street. A woman was looking at me, her eyes sad. She walked to me and bent down.

"I know just the woman for you, honey. She needs a puppy with those kinds of eyes. Come with me."

I knew what her words meant but I wasn't sure I wanted to. This was a city, a bad place. Bad things happened in those places.

The woman took out a black thing and started to talk into it.

"Damesha, please! I can't keep a dog in my apartment, but you're allowed pets!"

Who was Damesha? Was she nice? I followed the woman as she talked and we eventually stopped at a door.

She was beautiful! And magical too! A light shimmered around her, fading in and out, but it was her eyes that got my attention.

A piercing light blue, they were so similar to my Mommy's eyes, so kind, so in need of love.

Yes, this might be alright, after all. I looked behind me for a moment, wishing I could go back to *her*, but the light had said I couldn't. And that this life would be better.

I took a step into the room, my mind made up.

I went to the woman and nudged at her leg, wanting to get her attention. "You're so little, but somehow so big aren't you?"

The love in her eyes made me feel warm but a loud

noise frightened me, some kind of sound I'd never heard.

"It's okay, baby, it's only the kettle." The woman did some stuff, put some food down for me, and before long I was inspecting the new home I'd been given.

A few moments later the women were staring down at me, discussing things I could now perfectly understand. I needed a name, they said, but I had one. Besides, this rug had some magic on it and it wasn't a very nice rug. It had plans of tripping the one named Damesha. Maybe hurting her even!

"Annie?" The woman that smelled of love and friendship called out to me and I was utterly amazed. She knew my name. Oh yes, this was home for me, she was home for me now. I wouldn't forget my Mommy, I could never forget her, but this lady was like her in so many ways. As I perched on her knees and gave her a swipe of my tongue, I knew that I'd stick around for a little while. Even if she did say that word, travel. I hated traveling, but if it was with her, it might be alright. Besides, it would be an adventure right? I can understand the humans now, maybe I could even help, as the star-child had told me to do. I hoped I could, anyway.

The woman hugged me close and for a moment, I could feel my Mommy again. I miss her, but I have a new life now. I just hope she finds another star-child like me, in need of her love and devotion.

Shift Quickie

2 Hard To Bear

Bearly Over

Bearly Wolf

Kill Order

The Alpha

Kane

Cade

Jacob

Destiny Of The Dragon Prince

Defying The Dragon Prince

Chamber Of The Dragon Prince

His To Take

His to Mate

His To Save

and more…

ABOUT THE AUTHOR

Selina Coffey is a romance writer who lives happily in London with her husband and son. She is a hopeless romantic who grew up always believing in love and she is not ashamed to admit this! It is this belief that makes her so passionate about writing crazy love stories.

A stereotypical girly girl, she loves shopping. So whenever she gets a chance and the spare cash, you will probably find her browsing online for the next pair of shoes to add to her collection.

You can find her online at
www.selinacoffey.com

Contact her at
hello@selinacoffey.com

www.ingramcontent.com/pod-product-compliance
Lightning Source LLC
Chambersburg PA
CBHW051306210726
48287CB00002B/688